UNIVERSAL STUDIOS MONSTERS

Dracula™

RETURN OF EVIL

A TALE OF TERROR FOR THE 21st CENTURY

UNIVERSAL STUDIOS
MONSTERS

Dracula™

BY LARRY MIKE GARMON

SCHOLASTIC INC.

New York Toronto London Auckland Sydney
Mexico City New Delhi Hong Kong Buenos Aires

ISBN 0-439-20846-7

Designed by Peter Koblish

12 11 10 9 8 7 6 5 4 3 2   1 2 3 4 5 6/0
Printed in the U.S.A.

First Scholastic printing, August 2001

*Many thanks to Bonnie, who had faith, and for Beth,
who had patience.*
*This is for Charity, Shaune, Nicholas, and Lorry —
the angels of my better nature.*

CHAPTER ONE
LAST NIGHT — THIRTEEN SECONDS AFTER MIDNIGHT

"Lovely night for a murder!" Ralph Gentry yelled above the roar of the waves as they hit the side of the aluminum skiff.

"Yeah!" Todd, his son, shouted back. "Especially if your name's pompano or kingfish!" He jerked back on the fishing rod with all his strength.

"Don't try to set the hook too quickly, son!" his father shouted, turning in his seat to watch. "It could slip right out of the fish's mouth."

"I got it, Dad!" Todd yanked back on the fishing pole again, taking the slack out of the line. The fiberglass rod bowed into a semicircle, the tip nearly touching the dark ocean before it receded again. He felt a tug from the other end of the line. In his mind he pictured the sharp, barbed hook setting in the fleshy mouth of a gulf kingfish or an African pompano along the beach where he and his father had spent the last hour shore fishing.

He tilted the fishing pole forward, giving the line more slack. A tug from the other end told him that the hook was set and the fish was making a run for it. He quickly jerked the pole back. The line was taut and the pole bent into an arc again, the tip inches away from the surface of the black water.

"Here, let me help you." Mr. Gentry reached for the pole.

Todd turned away slightly from his father. "No. I can do this." His tone was not disrespectful; he just wanted to fight this fight by himself, to prove to his father that he had the strength, the desire, and the heart to defeat his foe. He turned his attention back to the pole and the fish at the end of the line. It was putting up a good fight. *Could be ten, fifteen pounds,* he thought. *Maybe a trophy.*

A dark cloud moved slowly in the heavens. Gradually, a bright silver sliver of the full moon peeked around the cloud. A few seconds later, the entire moon was visible in the midnight sky — a large, cold-looking orb, but the light it gave off lit up the shoreline in monochromatic shades of white, gray, and black.

"Here . . . it . . . comes!" Todd was turning the reel's handle as quickly as he could. He tilted the fishing pole forward. The fish on the other end of the line tugged with all its might as it tried to swim farther out into the ocean. Todd pulled the pole backward, setting the hook even deeper into the fish's flesh. Then he cranked the reel again.

"That's it, son. Pull it in!"

Todd groaned. The fish on the other end of the line wasn't going to give up without a fight. He pulled back on the rod, then lowered it and yanked back again. The strategy was to tire the fish, to weaken it, to sap every ounce of energy and spirit until it submitted to his will.

Father was encouraging son. Son was focusing on the fight with the fish. Neither noticed the ship drifting toward them from behind. It hit the skiff with a thud.

The skiff tilted to starboard, and both men spilled into the dark, cold ocean. They bounced on the water as their life jackets held their heads and shoulders above the surf.

The ship continued on its silent journey, pushing the skiff along and separating father and son.

"Dad!" Todd shouted, his hands cupped so his voice would carry over the vessel.

"I'm okay, Todd. What about you?"

"I'm all right."

The ship moved past them. Todd could now see his father some ten yards away. They swam toward each other.

"Where'd that come from?" Mr. Gentry said, watching the stern move away from them.

The ship — a fifty-foot luxury cruiser — drifted a few more yards and finally grounded itself in the sand of the shallow shore.

Todd and his dad swam toward it. When they

reached the stern's ladder, Mr. Gentry grasped on to the ladder's sides. "Hey on board!" he shouted. "On board!"

"Looks like the mooring line broke," Todd said, pointing to a ripped and ragged rope dangling from the starboard side of the boat.

"Hey! On board!" his father shouted once more. "What would a ship be doing drifting around here? The San Tomas Marina is fifteen miles away."

Todd knew that his father's question was rhetorical. "Maybe we ought to check it out. Find out why they cost me the biggest fish of my life."

"Whoever's on that ship better have a good explanation," Mr. Gentry said, laughing. He started up the ladder.

Todd had followed him up to the deck. "Anybody on board?" his father shouted.

"Probably just broke away from its mooring during the storm," Todd said.

"You're probably right."

The storm had hit the central east coast of Florida five hours earlier — a sudden summer storm that came and went in a matter of thirty minutes. But it had hit with all the fury and power of nature. Strong gusts had broken old trees in half, and power lines had snapped like dried spaghetti. Sections of San Tomas Inlet were still without power.

That's when Todd Gentry and his dad had decided to get in some late-night beach fishing at one of the estuaries just north of San Tomas Inlet. The fishing after such a storm would be excellent, and the estuary they had selected was one known for an abundance of large and delectable fish.

"What's that smell?" Todd asked as they reached the entryway to the ship's cabin.

"I'm not sure," Mr. Gentry replied. He grabbed the waterproof flashlight hooked onto the side of his belt, pushed the switch, and focused the beam down the ladder. Todd did the same. "Looks deserted."

They descended into what would have been a den in a home. The ship was indeed a luxury vessel—walnut paneling, gilded light fixtures, ceramic door handles, leather chairs. It was also a mess. The chairs were ripped and overturned. The cedar end tables had been reduced to broken boards and splinters. The floor was littered with books, paper, lamps, shredded cushions, and shattered glass.

"The storm really did some serious damage to this ship," Todd said.

"Well, the storm might have caused things to fall from the walls, but how did all this furniture get broken?"

Todd shrugged. His father was right. If the ship had been moored to a dock and torn away during the storm, the furnishings would have been strewn about, but they would not have been shattered and torn.

"Looks more like a battleground," Mr. Gentry said.

"Someone's insurance company is going to enjoy assessing this mess," Todd said. He could hear the gentle lapping of the waves against the ship's hull. Although reason told him the ship was empty, instinct told him to be on full alert. He kicked at some of the debris. "Maybe it was stolen and the thieves were trying to escape with it when the storm hit."

"Could be," Mr. Gentry said, guiding his flashlight's beam around the large room. "But where are they now?"

Todd shrugged again.

Suddenly, a low-pitched whine echoed through the cabin.

"What was that?" Mr. Gentry turned his flashlight on Todd.

Todd was in the middle of the cabin. He pointed his flashlight down a nearby passageway. The beam disappeared into the darkness.

The whine filled the cabin again.

"Someone's on board," Todd said.

"Sounds more like a dog," Mr. Gentry replied.

"Maybe the thieves left their dog behind."

"More likely the dog belongs to the owner, and the thieves locked him in one of the rooms." Mr. Gentry started down the passageway, pointing his flashlight from side to side.

The passageway was narrow, barely wide enough for Todd's broad shoulders. It, too, was covered with broken furniture, shards of glass, and shredded cushions.

"There's that smell again," Todd said.

"Yeah."

The whining filled the passageway, but now it came from behind them.

"Must be in one of the rooms we passed," Mr. Gentry said.

Todd turned. They had their choice of four doors, two on either side of the passageway.

"Take door number one," Mr. Gentry said. "But be careful: If it is a dog, it's probably scared and may attack."

Todd grabbed the doorknob, and turned it slowly. He opened the door a few inches, pointing the flashlight beam through the slit. He whistled softly. "Here, boy . . . or girl."

There was no sound in response. Todd swung the door open all the way. He gagged. The stench from the room was stifling. It hit his nostrils with a heated fury that made him hold his breath. He slammed the door shut.

"What is it?" Mr. Gentry asked.

"Something in that room smells dead!"

"Dead?"

"Yeah. Like three-day-old roadkill."

Mr. Gentry stepped past his son and opened the

door slightly. "Whew!" he said, grimacing. He quickly closed the door. "It's the galley," he said. "Probably just some rotten meat."

Todd opened the door directly across the passageway. The same putrid smell assailed his nostrils. He shut the door quickly. "Two galleys?"

"I wouldn't think so," Mr. Gentry said as he walked to the third door.

Something tickled the back of Todd's neck. It was a cold, metallic sensation that sent a shiver from the base of his skull down his spine. "Something's very wrong here." He turned, the flashlight's beam following his movement.

Mr. Gentry was just beginning to open the third door.

"No!" Todd cried. But his warning came too late: Mr. Gentry had opened the door.

The whine began just as Mr. Gentry turned the handle. It started as a low, high-pitched keening, but as Mr. Gentry pushed on the door, it became a low, guttural growl.

Mr. Gentry entered the room. Todd followed, thrusting his flashlight inside. The whine stopped as suddenly as it had begun. The beam illuminated a room in shambles, just like the den — broken furniture and lamps, shredded cushions everywhere.

Todd gagged again. But not from the smell of death. This time it was from the signs of death. The walls were stippled and daubed with blood as though some insane painter had been let loose with a paintbrush soaked in crimson. Todd leaned against the door frame for support.

Mr. Gentry was moving slowly about the cabin, his beam revealing broken furniture and tattered shirts and pillows.

"We've got to call the police," Todd said. "My cell phone's in the truck. Come on, let's go."

The whining began again, louder than before.

"Someone's in the closet," Mr. Gentry said. He walked the short distance to the louvered closet door. He held the light up to the slats and tried to peer through the narrow opening. The whining stopped. "I can't see anything."

"Let's go, Dad. We've got to call the police."

"Wait!" Mr. Gentry said. "Someone's in here. He's hurt." His hand grabbed the knob on the closet door.

"NO!" Todd dashed to the door; his free hand stretched out to slam it shut. But Mr. Gentry had the door fully open before Todd could reach him.

The pair stood in front of the dark opening, the beams of their flashlights soaking the inside of the closet with a blinding white light. Two luminous, almond-shaped objects shone out in the glare. They appeared to be under a bundle of clothes that had fallen from the closet's hangers. A low growl sounded from under the pile. Then the objects disappeared and reappeared almost as quickly. Like eyes blinking.

"Dad," Todd began softly — but he never got a chance to finish his sentence.

The bundle exploded and a large dog catapulted toward Mr. Gentry, hitting him with such force that the man was knocked into the air. He slammed into the bulkhead on the opposite side of the cabin.

"Dad!"

The dog was on top of the man in an instant. Mr. Gentry's free hand gripped the dog's throat while he swung the flashlight at its head.

"Dad!" Todd ran to his father, his flashlight raised. He hit the dog on its back haunches. The dog yelped and turned toward Todd.

For the first time, Todd could see the animal clearly. But it wasn't a dog. It was a wolf. The largest wolf Todd had ever seen. Four feet across at the shoulders. Its yellow eyes were set in a large, elongated head. Its ears were pinned back on its sloping forehead. Its black lips were curled over red-stained teeth.

Todd slowly backed away. He saw his father rise up from the floor and swing his flashlight at the wolf's hindquarters. The force of the blow spun the animal around.

"Run, Todd!" his father yelled. Then the wolf pounced on him, knocking Mr. Gentry back to the floor. His flashlight fell to the floor, spinning. It finally stopped so that the beam washed the pair in a brilliant arc of light, illuminating the battle between man and beast.

Todd lurched forward, swinging his flashlight. The growling and the snapping of the wolf's teeth filled the room. Todd heard his father groaning with pain.

"No, Todd! Run! Call for help!"

"No!" Todd yelled.

"Run! Get . . . help!"

Todd was battering the wolf with all his might, bringing the flashlight down on its head again and again. But his blows had no impact.

"RUN!"

Todd dove at the wolf's head. It swung around and caught Todd with a head butt. Todd staggered backward, dazed and blinded by the blow.

The wolf turned its attention back to Todd's father.

"Run . . . Todd . . . run."

Todd heard his father's voice through the rushing roar of pain. The voice was weak and soft.

"Run . . . Todd . . . run."

Todd stood on wobbly legs and staggered to the door. He fell into the passageway.

The wolf's growling grew louder.

Todd moved slowly down the passageway to the den, leaning against the bulkhead for support.

The snapping of the wolf's teeth echoed throughout the ship.

Todd pointed the beam of his flashlight across

the den to the ladder that led up to the deck. He stumbled over broken furniture and torn cushions, nearly falling as he strained to reach it.

An ear-piercing scream filled the ship. Then . . . Silence.

Todd reached the bottom of the ladder. He could hear the gentle lapping of the waves as they hit the listing ship.

He turned and pointed the beam of his flashlight across the den and into the passageway. His heart beat against his chest. His temples felt as though they would explode. His eyes were stinging from the sweat that dripped from his eyebrows. He wiped his eyes and focused them on the beam shining into the passageway.

The giant head of the wolf emerged into the passageway. The wolf slowly started down the passageway toward Todd. Its head was lowered, eyes fixed on its next prey, black lips curled over teeth wet with blood, reddish saliva drooling from the lower jaw.

Todd backed slowly up the ladder, keeping the beam of light in the wolf's eyes. He reached the top of the ladder and stood looking down into the den as the wolf stopped at the bottom of the ladder.

The wolf looked up at Todd. It put one paw on the bottom step of the ladder, then paused.

"Dad!" Todd called out.

Tiny waves hit the side of the ship.

"DAD!"

The wolf seemed to smile.

"DAAAAAD!"

The wolf bolted up the ladder.

Todd turned and ran to the bow of the ship. He jumped over the bow's railing and fell forward into the shallow surf. His head sunk under the water.

The cold water sparked a new urgency within him. Todd jumped to his feet and sprinted up the beach toward his pickup. He could hear a splash behind him. He reached the passenger side of the truck and pulled on the latch. It slipped under his wet hand. He yanked on it several more times before he realized the door was locked. He jammed his free hand into his jeans pocket and pulled out a set of keys. He shoved one into the lock and twisted the key with force.

But before he could open the door, the wolf was on him. Todd swung his flashlight, catching the wolf across the jaw. It fell to one side. Todd used the flashlight to smash the window. Reaching through the broken glass, he unlocked the door. He jumped into the truck's cab and fumbled with the key. He jammed it into the ignition and the engine roared to life.

The wolf's head appeared in the broken passenger window, its jaws snapping at him. Todd grabbed the flashlight and struck the wolf, knocking it away from the window. Simultaneously he stomped on the accelerator. The truck sped forward, the steering wheel spinning freely, guiding the truck back toward the black ocean. Todd grabbed the wheel and spun it around, nosing the truck to the concrete boat ramp.

The wolf appeared in the passenger window again, hanging on to the door with its forepaws. Todd raised and lowered the flashlight several times, striking the wolf on the muzzle and forehead. He spun the steering wheel to the left, and the truck hit the ramp. The wheels squealed as the rubber hit the asphalt.

Todd looked in the rearview mirror and saw the wolf roll for several yards. Then he saw it stand — not on all fours, as wolves are wont to do. No, the wolf stood on its hind legs, like a man.

Todd turned his attention to the road. His eyes stung with sweat and tears. He grabbed his cell phone and punched the emergency number.

Back on the beach, the wolf watched as the truck's red taillights disappeared in the distance. It turned and started walking back to the ship. The wolf looked up at the full moon and bathed in its reflected light. He felt the transformation begin — hair receding, nose flattening, leg bones elongating into human bones, paws stretching forth into fingers. By the time he reached the water's edge, he was half man, half wolf.

A black object at the water's edge caught his eye. He reached down with long, hairy fingers and grabbed the object.

A wallet. He flipped it open. Todd Gentry smiled up at him from a driver's license. He flipped through the photos. Todd and school buddies. Todd and the older man now lying on the boat. Todd and a girl. And then a single photo of the same girl.

A girl with blond hair, bright-blue eyes, and an alluring smile. A girl whose beauty stirred within him an ancient loneliness. Faded, distant memories shimmered just below the surface of his confused and foggy mind.

He looked around. This wasn't his world. Not the world he had known. This world was bright and had textures and sounds and shades he had never seen before. He didn't know where he was.

He looked down at the picture again. He was in a strange world, but the woman was no stranger. Mina — the woman for whom he spent eternity looking. It was she who would bring peace and love to his tortured soul.

The beautiful young woman with blond hair and blue eyes smiled up at him. He touched the photograph softly. A hint of a smile played around his cruel red lips.

Then the half man, half wolf raised his head to the sky, and a howl of desolation filled the night. He transformed completely into human — a full-grown man with jet-black hair, bloodred eyes, translucent skin, and large, white teeth. He tore the photo from the plastic sleeve and tossed the wallet aside. He looked at it again, the pain of loneliness boiling through his corrupt blood.

In the blink of an eye, the man had changed into a giant bat. He sailed into the pitch-black night, silhouetted against the dull, gray full moon.

CHAPTER TWO
SAME NIGHT, SIX HOURS EARLIER

"Don't make a sound. If you make any noise at all, evil will hear you and you may not get out alive." The old man laughed, raised his hands and arms menacingly, and leaned closer to the three teenagers standing across from him. The laugh was a high-pitched cackle, like fingernails on a chalkboard.

The three teens looked at the man and then at one another. The shortest of the three shrugged and said, "Well, I guess we'll just have to die." He echoed the old man's laugh, a large, toothy smile on his round face.

The other teens snickered. The old man frowned. Bob Hardin had that effect on people: Kids thought he was funny; adults thought he was annoying.

"You want the projector or don't ya?" The old man stood with his arms crossed, frowning.

"Yes, Mr. Brown," the biggest of the teens said.

"Captain Bob here just has his hat on too tight." Joe Motley grabbed the cap off Bob's head.

"Hey! Give that back!"

Joe held the hat in the air high over Bob's head. Bob jumped as high as he could, reaching for it. But with Joe's height and arm length, Bob was doing little more than swatting at air.

"Okay, kids. Let's settle down or you won't get recess." At sixteen, Nina Nobriega was the oldest of the three teens. She sighed and shook her head. Sometimes she felt as if she ought to get paid for baby-sitting Bob and Joe instead of just being friends with them.

Nina had met the boys at the beginning of the summer, when the three had won internships at the Universal Studios Florida theme park in Orlando. She was surprised to learn that both boys were only fourteen because she distinctly remembered reading on the application that only high school students sixteen and over would be considered for the coveted positions.

Nina soon became friendly with the two freshmen and discovered they all had three things in common: high IQs, near-expert skill with computers, and an interest in the classic horror movies of Universal Studios.

At first she thought Joe, who stood six-one, was a senior in high school. He was certainly the biggest fourteen-year-old she had ever seen. He also had a more mature attitude than most high school freshmen.

"Give . . . me . . . back . . . my . . . hat!" Bob continued to swat at air as he reached for his hat.

Well, sometimes Joe was more mature than boys his age. For reasons she had yet to figure out, Nina had observed that whenever Joe was around Bob, his maturity level went down a couple of notches.

Bob — Captain Bob, as he liked to be called — was a work in progress. With his intelligence and wit, he would either be a successful comedian or a politician; she hadn't figured out which. And that name he insisted on everyone calling him: Captain Bob. Only Joe ever really used it. From Joe she had learned that Bob had adopted the nickname when his favorite uncle had given him a worn-out yacht captain's hat. It was black, tattered, and had definitely seen better days, but Bob wouldn't go anywhere without it.

"Give . . . it . . . back."

"Do you want the pro-jec-tor or not?" Mr. Brown still had his arms folded and a frown on his face.

"Come on, Joe," Nina said. "We don't have time for this."

Joe let the hat drop just as Bob was in mid-leap. It hit him in the face.

"Thanks . . . pal." Bob put the hat firmly on his head, pulling it down behind his ears.

"Yes, Mr. Brown," Nina began. "We'd like the projector."

"Then let's move along, kids." Mr. Brown held up a large key ring.

"Wow! Must be a thousand keys on that thing!" Bob reached for it.

"Uh-uh, sonny. Adults only."

Bob smirked. "We're *young* adults."

Mr. Brown selected a long, silver key from the hundreds on the ring and slid it into the door's lock. There was a metallic click, and then a snap echoed through the concrete hallway. The heavy metal door swung open, the hinges creaking.

"All right," Bob said as he headed toward the opening, rubbing his hands together.

Mr. Brown stopped Bob with a hand on the boy's chest. "Now, you kids promise to have this thing back Sunday afternoon?"

"Yeah, sure," Bob said.

Mr. Brown looked at Nina and raised his eyebrows.

"Yes, Mr. Brown. I promise to have the projector back Sunday afternoon."

"Well then, it's all yours. Enjoy." He laughed again with that nails-on-chalkboard cackle and disappeared down the concrete hallway, his footfalls echoing softly.

"Jeez!" Captain Bob commented. "He's got all the personality of a piece of moldy cheese."

"Come on," Nina said, pushing past Bob and flipping on the light switch. They walked into a large, dimly lit storage room. Rows of metal shelves ran from the floor to the ceiling. "Let's grab the projector and get out of here."

"This is gonna be cool," Joe said, following Nina.

"Let's get it and split," Bob said in a harsh whisper. "We don't want to get caught."

"Caught?" Nina said. "Thought you said you had permission to borrow it."

Joe frowned at Bob. "I do." He started scanning the shelves. "Mr. Tanner in R and D said they needed somebody to test the projector at home. They've done all the controlled experiments and now they need some real-life situations to work out any bugs they may've missed in the lab."

"Bugs? What bugs? You know I hate bugs!" Captain Bob looked around his feet, ready to stomp on any six-legged creature in sight. He loved quoting old horror flicks at every opportunity that presented itself.

Nina sighed. "Oh, brother."

When Joe had first told her and Bob about the projector, she hadn't believed it. The internships at Universal Studios were designed to give teenagers who had an interest in moviemaking an opportunity to work beside the creators and engineers of the park's exhibits. Nina had been assigned to *Alfred Hitchcock: The Art of Making Movies*, while Captain Bob was delighted to be working at *The Gory, Gruesome, and Grotesque Horror Makeup Show.*

Joe received the best assignment of all, at the Research and Development department. He was little more than a gofer, but he got to observe the artists, engineers, and scientists who created, designed, and constructed the Universal Studios worldwide theme parks. It was in the R&D department that Joe had first heard of the projector.

Not just any projector. A projector that would change home entertainment in the same way the Internet had changed world communications.

Known by its nickname, the "hair dryer," the projector was chrome-plated silver, and did, indeed, look like a gigantic hair dryer. It had a long tapering nozzle at one end and a round housing unit at the other. Joe explained to his friends that the projector was designed to hang from the ceiling and project the movie into the center of the room. What made the projector so special was that it could show any movie in three dimensions — without special glasses. The image of the movie was fed into the hair dryer through a SCSI computer connection attached to a newly developed video/soundboard developed by Universal Studios R&D. All movies had to be digitized on special DVD disks and played through the computer's special movie media player.

Joe explained that the hair dryer projected a hologram of the characters in the movie. Viewers could not interact with the characters, but they could get a more realistic experience from the movie and could watch it from any angle. It was like seeing a high-tech stage version of the movie. Joe also said he had permission to "borrow" the projector for the weekend.

So the three friends had planned to spend the weekend viewing their favorite classic horror films: the original versions of *Dracula*, *The Wolf Man*, *Frankenstein*, *The Mummy*, *Creature from the Black Lagoon*, and *The Bride of Frankenstein*. Captain Bob had already burned the horror films onto special DVD disks, while Nina had added the new SCSI video–soundboard to her home computer and uploaded the special media player.

The plan was to get the projector on Friday afternoon, when they got off work; drive back to their hometown, San Tomas Inlet, which was only forty miles east of Orlando; and spend Friday night watching the first three horror classics and Saturday night watching the final three. On Sunday afternoon, they'd return the projector to the studio, as they had promised Mr. Brown.

As Nina, Joe, and Bob searched the storeroom for the projector, they could hear footsteps echoing in the concrete hallway.

"Someone's coming," Captain Bob whispered.

"Let's find this thing and get out of here," Joe whispered back.

"Why are we whispering?" Nina whispered. "We have permission, don't we?"

Joe wasn't listening to Nina. He was moving

quickly through the rows of shelves, scanning up and down, looking for the projector.

Captain Bob peered down the hallway. His eyes widened. A large figure was coming toward them, each step deliberate and determined. "Someone really is coming!" he whispered.

"I can't find it!" Joe whispered.

"What's going on, guys?" Nina was starting to have a bad feeling about this. She had visions of her summer job being flushed down the toilet.

"Hurry, Joe. He's a big fella."

Bob could tell that the man was taller than Joe. He was silhouetted against the hallway light. He also looked strong. But the strangest thing was that the man looked as though he had two knobs sticking out of either side of his neck.

"Joe, Joe, Joe," Captain Bob said quickly.

Joe trotted up and down the aisles, his head jerking up and down, his eyes focusing and refocusing on the name tags below each object on the shelf. "Got it!" he said suddenly. He grabbed the large chrome "hair dryer," tucked it under his shirt, and started toward the door.

"Why are you hiding it?" Nina asked.

"We have to protect the lens from moisture and sunlight," Joe replied.

"Well, it's not raining and we're indoors."

"Hey, guys and gals," Captain Bob whispered. "It's time to get out of here."

The footfalls of the approaching man grew

louder. Captain Bob could hear his heavy breathing. He turned to Nina and Joe. "I'm off, said the madman."

Nina rolled her eyes at hearing Captain Bob's signature exit line. "Let's go," she said to Joe. "But we're going to talk about this on the drive home."

"Yeah. Whatever you say," Joe said. "Let's just get out of here."

Nina and Joe ran into the hallway. Captain Bob was already at the other end, waiting for them.

"Hurry up, you two!" he shouted as he waved at his friends. "The monster is going to kill you!" Then he disappeared through the exit.

Nina and Joe didn't pause to look back at whoever was in the hallway; they just followed Bob's cue and ran out the door.

Mr. Brown walked down the hallway holding a large cardboard cutout of Frankenstein in front of him. He reached the open storage room door. "Crazy kids," he muttered. "Can't even shut a door when they're done."

He walked into the storage room and stood the cardboard display against a wall. Then he walked down an aisle and stopped about midway. He scratched his gray head.

"Crazy kids," he muttered, picking up an exact replica of the 3-D projector Joe had snagged. "They took the broken prototype instead of the working model."

CHAPTER THREE
SAME NIGHT, SEVEN P.M.

"Hey! Who ordered the blood?"

"You drop and break that bottle on my mom's new white carpet, and she'll be calling for *your* blood." Nina stood in the middle of her family's entertainment room, looking back toward the food counter.

Bob was stooped at the mini-refrigerator, waving a bottle of catsup back and forth. As he stood, the bottle slipped from his hands. "Whoops!"

"Bob!" Nina sprinted across the room. Logically she knew she could not have covered the twenty feet in time to catch the bottle and keep it from spilling on her mother's new white carpet, but her reaction was more instinctual than rational.

Bob quickly dropped to one knee and caught the white plastic top with his right thumb and index finger. The bottle swung back and forth like a pendulum. "Quick as ever."

Nina grabbed the bottle from him. "I ought to bean you with this!"

"Hey, I was only kidding," Bob protested. "I wouldn't really have dropped it."

"Some joke. If my folks get back from the movies and find this place a mess, I'll be grounded." Nina set the bottle on the counter next to the hamburgers she had just cooked. "My mom would skin you and me alive. And then she would do something *really* terrible to us."

"Almost ready," Joe announced. He sat at the computer desk, his eyes fixed on the screen as binary codes and commands rolled past him. He was oblivious to the exchange between Nina and Bob. "I've just tweaked the program so we can adjust the clarity and focus using the VCR remote."

Nina walked toward the loveseat, a plate of chopped-up hamburger, french fries, and sliced pickles in one hand and a glass of iced tea in the other. On the way home, she had gotten Joe to confess that he had not really received permission to borrow the projector. Mr. Tanner had said that Joe could examine the projector and perhaps even set it up in one of the viewing rooms — but not that he could take it outside the studio lot. Nina had almost turned her car around and headed back to the theme park. Joe had apologized for the deception and convinced her to at least look at one of the films, and then they could take it back the next morning. They were already on the outskirts of San Tomas Inlet and she was curious about the projector, so she'd reluctantly agreed.

"You put the disks in the jukebox?" Nina asked Bob.

"Ya. I di." Bob tried to speak, but his mouth was jammed with hamburger and fries and he was trying to wash it down with a swig of Mountain Dew — all at the same time.

"You know," Nina said, watching Bob, "you give gross a bad name."

"Ya. A't i' cool?" Bob mumbled.

"Yes," Joe said as he continued to type commands into the program. "He put all six movies in the DVD jukebox." He poked the ENTER key with his right pinky. "There!" He swiveled around in the chair. "It's show time!"

"Ya ga u surge on?" Bob asked, chomping away.

Nina scrunched up her face in disgust.

"Yeah, Bob," Joe said. "The surger's on."

As if on cue, the early evening sky lit up with lightning.

"It's just a small storm about two miles off the coast," Joe explained. "It'll pass. You do the honors." He tossed the remote to Nina.

Joe took a seat in the big recliner. Nina was sitting on a love seat across from him. Bob had parked himself on the couch. The projector hung from a small hook in the ceiling, the silver nozzle pointed at the center of the room.

"Turn out the lights," Nina told Bob, just as he took another bite of his hamburger. Catsup dribbled down the side of his mouth as he stood up. Nina sighed. "Never mind, burger boy." She hit the switch herself.

With the lights off, the room was almost completely dark. An occasional lightning strike at sea cast quick shadows across the floor, and a rising full moon pitched in just enough gray light to give the room a slightly sinister look.

"Here goes nothing," Nina said, pressing the PLAY button.

They sat in silence for a momemt before they heard the hum of the DVD drive. Then a slight flicker flashed from the end of the projector. White blobs floated in the center of the room.

"Adjust the focus!" Bob shouted.

"Now it speaks clearly," Nina said, rolling her eyes. She pressed a button on the remote and the blobs took shape.

Three-dimensional letters floated a few feet off the floor. They formed the word *Dracula*.

"Yea!" Bob and Joe shouted, clapping.

Even the music projected through Nina's surround-sound system seemed more clear and distinct. Everyone forgot about their food and watched in awe as the three-dimensional figures acted out the tragic and horrible life of Count Dracula. Once Nina thought that the Count was actually reaching out to touch her.

Captain Bob let out an ear-piercing scream when

the Count transformed himself into a bat and flew off into the night — right at Captain Bob's head and his beloved hat. "Take that!" he yelled as he took a couple of swipes at the three-dimensional bat.

"Sit down, Bob," Nina said wearily.

Bob jumped into the middle of the room and pretended to act with the characters.

"Sit down!"

"This is too cool." Bob was dancing around the three-dimensional holograms. "It's like they're ghosts or something."

Every time Bob tried to grab a character, his hand would pass through it. He even stepped "into" a character and walked around, pretending to be part of the movie, the ghostly image of the character covering his body like a see-through shroud.

A pillow hit Bob in the face, knocking his hat off. "I said *sit down*," Nina said again. She'd been kidding before, but now she was starting to get irritated.

"Jeez!" Bob said, picking up his hat. "You're a lousy movie date."

"A date?" Nina said with a laugh. "You've got some ego."

Bob returned to the couch. "What do you mean by that?"

"Will you two be quiet," Joe said with exasperation. He was busy marveling at the technology. The images were so clear, they looked like real people acting on a stage, only in black-and-white. He had to keep telling himself that he was watching a movie, not a live performance.

They were all so engrossed in the film that none of them noticed that the "little" storm that was supposed to have stayed out on the Atlantic Ocean had turned landward and transformed itself into a late summer gale. The room was suddenly awash in brilliant light. A clap of thunder followed a split second later, and the windows of the room rattled.

Captain Bob jumped up from the couch. "What was that?"

Another lightning strike and a bang of thunder — and then thunderous blows of heavy rain on the windows and roof.

"Are we in a hurricane warning?" Nina asked.

"No," Joe said. "It was just supposed to be a small squall."

"Hey! He's a poet and he don't —"

"Not now, Bob!" Nina ran to the sliding glass doors. Lightning lit up the sky, the ocean, and the beach that was Nina's backyard. The clouds were thick and dark. "That's no small squall."

"Unplug everything," Joe commanded.

All three dived toward the nearest outlets to pull out the electrical plugs. But they were too late. A fiery bolt of electricity hit the electrical pole that fed the house. The charge surged down the thick electrical wire and into the fuse box. It sizzled and then exploded, but not before the internal current divided itself among the various circuit breakers and, with the speed of light, hit every outlet in the house.

"Look!" Captain Bob yelled above the thunder and the rain.

The three-dimensional figure of Dracula wavered. The vampire's face showed pain and surprise. His eyes glowed a bright white. His mouth opened and closed, but no words came out. He looked straight into Nina's eyes.

Nina felt a chill run down her spine. The figure reached out toward her face. His pale bony fingers were inches away from her. Nina was mesmerized by the vampire's stare. He leaned forward, his mouth opening to reveal long, razor-sharp fangs. Nina wanted to scream, but she couldn't. For just a fraction of a second, Nina felt the icy touch of living death.

The projector exploded. The rear hub threw sparks around the room. Nina screamed and covered her head. Shards of glass from the lens hit Joe and Captain Bob. The vampire had disappeared.

"Run for cover!" Bob yelled.

He and Joe ducked behind the sofa. Nina took shelter behind the love seat. She peeked over the edge and watched as the projector spewed sparks and sizzles and hisses.

A dazzling white light spilled from the nozzle end of the projector. It was more like a cascade of water than a beam of light. It gushed out in streams of white and gray and black, spreading across the new white carpet like water from a bottomless pitcher.

"What's happening?" Nina yelled.

"I don't know," Joe replied.

"This is fantastic!" Bob chimed in.

Then as suddenly as it had begun, the stream stopped. The room was quiet.

Nina, Joe, and Bob slowly rose. They looked at the center of the room just below the dead projector.

Swirls of white, gray, and black covered the carpet, mixing together as though they were in some slow-moving blender.

"Your mother is going to be really mad," Bob said.

Then the projector exploded one last time, sending the three teens scrambling for cover again. The explosion was loud, shattering a window and their soda glasses.

After several seconds, Joe stood up. "Is everyone okay?"

"Yes," Nina said. She rose from behind her chair.

"I think I ripped my pants," Bob said. He stood, turned, and checked his backside. "Yep. Ripped."

Nina carefully made her way to the kitchenette and pulled a flashlight from a drawer. She pointed the beam into the room.

"Hey!" Captain Bob shouted. "What happened to that big pool of . . . of . . . whatever? You saw it. What was that?"

"I don't know," Joe said. "Looked like a pool of liquid light."

Nina remained silent, tears welling in her eyes.

Bob had been right. Her mother would be upset. Food, drink, and smoldering bits of metal littered the new white carpet. She'd be grounded until she was thirty — and she'd be paying for the carpet out of her allowance for just as long.

Why did I ever get mixed up with these boys? Nina asked herself despairingly.

CHAPTER FOUR
ONE MONTH LATER — TUESDAY
LUNCH, PONCE DE LEON HIGH SCHOOL

"Angela. Wait up." Nina scurried across the wide lawn in front of Ponce de Leon High School, adjusting the books in her arms. She was trying to catch up with her friend. "Angela!" She reached the girl whose name she'd been calling and grabbed her by the shoulder. "Angela!"

"What?" Angela Chavarria cried out as she spun around. "Oh, it's you."

Nina looked into her friend's distant eyes. "Didn't you hear me calling you?"

"No. I guess I was thinking."

"What are you doing for lunch?"

Angela shrugged. "I don't know."

"I have an extra apple and a granola bar. Want to join me?"

Angela didn't answer. She was staring at the ground.

"Angela?" Nina said softly.

Angela shook her head. "I'm okay. Sure. Not really hungry, though."

They walked toward the grassy commons on the north side of the high school. Many students ate lunch there. Some listened to CDs, others studied, and some just took a quick nap before the beginning of afternoon classes.

Nina had known Angela since junior high school. The Chavarrias had moved to San Tomas Inlet after Angela's father retired from the United States Navy. Nina and Angela had become friends the first day of school and had remained close ever since.

"What are you doing Wednesday night?" Nina said, taking a bite of her apple.

"Probably nothing. As usual."

Nina offered her the granola bar. Angela shook her head.

"We've got a four-day break from school. Want to come over and spend the night?"

Angela sighed. "I don't know. Mom and Dad are going to New Orleans for a few days to hunt for some antiques for their shop. Mom wants me to take care of the fish tanks and feed the cat."

"What about your sister? Can't she do all that?"

"You mean Ms. Goth?" Angela smiled. "Devin doesn't get up before dark, and she's gone all night. Must be nice to be an adult."

"At least go to the movies with me or something. You've got to get out sometime."

"Yeah. I guess." Angela's eyes glazed over, and Nina could tell her friend was lost in thought once more.

"Hey, ladies!" Captain Bob yelled, throwing himself on the grass between the two girls.

"Go away, Bob. We're trying to have a conversation here," Nina protested.

"I can converse."

"An *intelligent* conversation."

"Oh, oh, my heart." Bob rolled onto his back, grabbing his chest. "It doth hurteth mucheth from thou slanderous razor tongueth."

Angela giggled.

"Hey. She's alive," Bob said. He had seen the girl around campus, but didn't know she was a friend of Nina's. "The name's Bob. Captain Bob." He lifted his captain's hat and nodded.

"I'm Angela. Nina's friend."

"Any friend of Nina's is a friend of Captain Bob's." Bob smiled and winked.

"Oh, brother. Don't you have some bugs to collect or rocks to examine or something to do other than bother us?" Nina asked.

"Nah," Bob said. "Dr. Franklin gave us until next month to finish our bug collection for biology, and I finished my rock collection and identification last night."

Nina looked at Bob, threatening him with her eyes.

"Hey, you gonna finish that?" Bob grabbed the half-eaten apple and took a bite.

"Not anymore." Nina turned to Angela and rolled her eyes. "Freshmen." She turned back to Bob. "I thought you ate in the cafeteria."

"Not today. They're serving UFOs." Bob bit into the apple.

"UFOs?" Angela said, brushing back a lock of blond hair.

"Unidentified Food Objects," Bob replied. "Hey! Joe! Over here!"

Joe waved and joined the group, plopping down next to Bob. "I was looking for you guys. I've got something to tell you."

"You know Angela?" Bob said to Joe, nodding toward her.

"Hi," Joe said to Angela. "Yeah. You're in my Algebra II class."

"Yeah," Angela said. "What's a freshman doing in Algebra II?"

Bob rubbed the top of Joe's head affectionately. "Boy's got brains shooting out all over him."

"Knock it off," Joe warned Bob, reaching for his hat. Bob ducked and scooted away. "Look, I got something to tell you guys. It's about those murders on I-95."

"Oh, yeah? I heard something about that on the radio this morning." Bob continued munching on the apple.

"I really don't want to hear this while I'm eating," Nina said.

"But you're not eating anything," Bob said.

"You know what I mean."

"Listen, guys. We could have a real mystery going on here. Not movie stuff — real life-and-death stuff!" Joe's eyes jumped with excitement. He sat up on his knees. "Last night I was over at Mike Turner's house —"

"Your cop friend?" Bob asked.

"Yeah. Detective Turner's sponsoring our forensics club after school. He's teaching us about how to investigate and look for clues at the crime scene. Turner's been helping the Florida Highway Patrol and state bureau of investigation with those three murders just outside of town."

"Why do they have a local cop helping them?"

Nina looked at Angela. Her friend had turned pale, and sweat beaded on her forehead. "Hey, guys. I don't think this is the right time —"

"Because the HP and bureau boys think that some cult could be operating around here —"

"In San Tomas Inlet?" Bob asked, excited.

"Yeah. A cult. Ain't that cool? Turner told me stuff that the newspapers don't even know."

"Joe," Nina said.

"Like what?" Bob said.

"Like each of the three victims was not much older than us —"

"Joe," Nina repeated, louder this time.

"— and each of the three victims died at night —"
"Joe!"

"— and each of the three victims looked like they had been attacked by a wolf or a cougar —"

"Cool. What else?" Bob took another bite of apple.

"— and each of the three victims had had the blood drained out of them!"

An ear-piercing scream startled Bob and Joe so much that both leaped to their feet. They looked around only to discover that the scream had come from Angela. Now she had her face buried in her hands.

"Are you two happy?" Nina shouted at the boys.

"What?" Bob said, holding his arms out in protest. "What did I do now?"

Angela sobbed softly.

"You two insensitive pinheads." Nina put her arm around Angela.

"What did I do?" Bob repeated, looking to Joe for support. Joe shrugged his shoulders.

Angela's head jerked up, and she looked up at Bob. Her puffy red eyes were slits of anger. "How can you think people getting killed is cool?" She stood, pushed through Bob and Joe, and stormed off.

"Jeez! Women!" Bob said, watching Angela. Nina slapped him on the shoulder. "Ow! What was that for?"

"For being a bigger jerk than you normally are!"

Bob looked at Joe again; Joe shrugged again.

"For two boys who are supposed to be geniuses, you two can be real idiots sometimes. Angela Chavarria? Remember what happened the night of the storm, when the projector blew up?"

Bob and Joe looked at each other. Then, as though someone had flipped a switch connected to both their brains, their faces lit up in understanding. "Oh, yeah," they said simultaneously.

"Yeah, that's right. Now you understand why I wanted you to stop, Joe?"

"I forgot," Joe said, looking down. His face turned red. He looked at Nina. "I'll tell her I'm sorry."

"I think I better handle this."

"Did they ever find out what happened with her boyfriend?" Joe asked.

"No," Nina began. "At least not anything from him. He hasn't spoken since they found him in his father's truck in a ditch."

"What's his name?" Joe said.

"Todd Gentry."

"What about his dad?" Bob said.

"He's still in a coma. He lost so much blood that they thought he was dead at first."

"Weird," Bob said. He took another bite of the apple. Then his eyes lit up. "Hey! Do you think the attack on the boat and the three murders are connected?"

"That's the other thing I wanted to tell you guys." Joe leaned closer to his friends and whispered, "Detective Turner says this is top secret. The first murders happened the night after the attack on the boat. According to Turner, Todd said he and his dad were attacked by a giant wolf."

"I thought the papers said that Todd was in a state of shock and hasn't spoken since that night," Nina said.

"That's right. But the people who found Todd said he was babbling on about a giant wolf walking on its hind legs like a man."

"Like a man?" Bob bit into the core of the apple, grimaced, and spit the bitter seeds out.

"Weird, huh?"

"Todd was already in shock," Nina said. "It's possible a wolf or maybe a cougar attacked them, like the other victims. But not one that walked around upright like a man."

"All I know is what Detective Turner told me," Joe said. "He said the freak storm that hit that night might have driven some wild animals from the nature preserve."

"What about the blood?" Bob said.

"That's where it really gets weird." Joe leaned in closer to his friends and whispered, "All three victims had teeth marks on their necks, like the attacker had bitten them. Every ounce of blood was drained from all three victims. Not drained out on the ground through their wounds. Drained out through their necks, through two pencil-sized holes surrounded by teeth marks. Like someone had sucked the blood out —"

"— and drank it!" Captain Bob finished.

CHAPTER FIVE
11:30 TUESDAY EVENING

"Too much blood. I need suction."

"Yes, Doctor." Devin Chavarria grabbed a thin plastic tube capped with a silver hooked tube and placed it in the patient's mouth. Immediately, the tube began suctioning out blood and saliva.

"Thank you," the dentist said, without looking up from his patient's mouth.

Devin did not say "You're welcome." She had been taught in dental hygienist school that the only time a dentist's assistant should speak is when something was wrong or when asked a direct question by the dentist.

What a change, Devin thought. *Not long ago, nothing would have kept me from speaking my mind about anything.*

Devin grabbed a white paper towel and dabbed up a bit of blood-tinged saliva that had dribbled from the corner of the patient's mouth. The dentist continued drilling into the patient's tooth. Root canals always took such a long time.

Three years earlier, Devin thought she'd known all the answers to life. She knew them so well that she had dropped out of school and hit the road with her boyfriend and his Goth metal band. At first, it was an adventure, an opportunity to get out of the yuppie-infested resort town of San Tomas Inlet. Slice, the name her boyfriend had adopted for himself, had promised her that he and Solid Flesh, his band, would soon hit the big time and they'd be living the life of multimillionaire rock stars.

Six months and a thousand miles later, Devin found herself in a roach-infested motel room, starving, with all her college savings gone. Slice was gone, too. He and his band mates left one night to go to a gig. Devin had felt sick and had stayed behind at the motel. But Slice and the band never returned, leaving Devin to pay the bill.

Fortunately, Devin's parents were understanding and invited her back home. But they had four conditions: Devin had to live at home, get her GED, go to technical college, and stay away from Slice.

Devin had kept all her promises — at least for a couple of years. Slice had reappeared in San Tomas Inlet a year earlier, and Devin had begun seeing him again.

Well, three out of four isn't bad.

Slice had returned shortly after she had graduated from dental hygienist school and had started working at the night emergency dental clinic along the San Tomas Inlet Beach Walk. Her parents did not know she was seeing Slice, but her younger sister, Angela, did.

The root canal was finished within the hour and the patient sent on his way.

"Let's call it a night," the dentist said to Devin, nodding to the clock just as it ticked midnight.

The San Tomas Inlet Night Dental Clinic had originally been conceived to handle nightly dental emergencies during the tourist season. But it soon began seeing regular patients who could not schedule a daytime appointment. It opened at four in the afternoon and took patients until midnight.

"You're the boss," Devin said with a smile. She picked up a clipboard. "No more appointments for tonight."

Devin liked the hours. Although she was now a hardworking, tax-paying citizen, she still clung to her Goth lifestyle: dyed jet-black hair, bright-red lipstick, black-painted fingernails, and dark clothing. And she liked staying out of the sun. Part of it had to do with her belief that too much sun was bad for you, and part of it had to do with her desire to make herself as pale as possible so her white skin would stand out against her black clothing.

Sometimes the patients would eye her suspiciously, but their stares and judgmental looks didn't bother her. She liked her job, and she liked the dentist with whom she was now working.

Dr. Abel Dunn had been at the clinic just a month now, but he was already popular with the patients and the other dental assistants. Not only was he a good dentist, he was young and handsome, and Devin made sure to be scheduled to work when Dr. Dunn was on duty. He was everything Slice wasn't.

Slice! Devin looked at her watch. 12:10. She was supposed to meet him at the Umbra Club in five minutes. The all-night punk-rock club was located just a few hundred yards from the night dental clinic.

"I'm leaving now, Doctor," she said, grabbing her large black purse.

"Call me Abel." Abel Dunn stood in the doorway between the waiting room and the hallway.

"I'm leaving now, Doct — Abel," Devin said with a smile.

"Lock up, please?"

"Sure, Doc — Abel." She began digging through the oversized bag for the keys.

"Hot date?"

"Just meeting Slice at the club."

"I see." He turned and started walking down the hallway.

In her haste, Devin dropped her bag. It hit the floor with a thud, spilling its contents everywhere. "OH!" Devin knelt down and began shoveling her stuff back in.

A shadow fell over her. Devin glanced up.

"Let me help you," Abel said, kneeling.

"Thank you, Doctor. I mean, Abel."

"Quite a bag of goodies you have," Abel said, gathering up lipstick cases, a brush, a couple of compacts, two address books, several CDs, and a pack of gum.

"I know," Devin said. Her face reddened. She took the items from Abel and placed them into her bag.

"Hey, what's this?" Abel held up a pocket-sized booklet with a colorful plastic cover. "Thought you only went for the dark and mysterious."

"Pictures." She reached for the photo album.

Abel did not hand the album to her. "May I look at it?" He flipped the album open.

Devin glanced at her watch. She would be late. Slice would be angry.

She looked at the dentist. At twenty-three, Abel was only two years older than she was. He had explained that he was a child prodigy who chose dentistry over medicine. He was a head taller than her, with long, shoulder-length black hair that he kept combed straight back and pulled into a ponytail when he worked on patients. His eyes were so dark they were almost black. Dr. Dunn — Abel — could be a model for the covers of the romance novels her sister read all the time.

Slice would be angry, but Devin did not care. Perhaps it was time to finally call it quits with him. Perhaps Dr. Dunn — Abel — would ask her . . .

"Who's this?" Abel held the photo album toward her.

Devin blushed when she saw the picture. "Oh, that's me and my kid sister at Halloween about ten years ago. Angela was a baby kitten and I was a witch."

"You make a beautiful witch," Abel said, his eyes locking on hers.

Devin felt her face turn hot. "Thanks."

Abel continued flipping through the photos. Devin began putting the rest of the items back into her purse. She turned around, looking for the keys that would lock the clinic's front door. She saw them under a chair a few feet away. She crawled to the chair and grabbed them. Then she turned back to tell Abel that she really had to leave. What she saw made her gasp silently.

Abel was sitting crossed-legged on the floor, holding the photo album in front of him. Although his head was tilted slightly down, she could still see his eyes. However, instead of the dark, dreamy eyes she admired, Abel's eyes were turned up, showing only the whites pulsing with tiny blood vessels.

"Doctor?" Devin crawled over to the dentist. "Doctor? Are you okay?" She grabbed his shoulders and slightly shook him. His shirt was soaked with sweat. "Abel!"

Abel shivered. His eyes rolled down, revealing the dark irises again. He shook his head.

"Abel?"

He looked up at Devin and smiled. "I'm okay. I must just be tired."

"What happened? Are you okay?" She took the open photo album from him and helped him stand with her free hand.

"Just tired," he explained. "Been working long hours. I suddenly felt exhausted, like I was going to pass out. Maybe it's the heat, I don't know."

"Want me to drive you home?"

"No," he said. "I'm okay. Really. Been working long nights, that's all."

"Are you sure?"

Abel smiled again — a smile that brought a calm to Devin. Perhaps she was overreacting. Something about Abel made her want to care for him.

"You go on your date. I'll be okay. Good night." He started off down the hallway.

"Good night, Doctor." Devin watched as he went into his office and shut the door.

Devin sighed, turned, and left the waiting room, locking the clinic's door behind her. She'd started toward the Umbra Club when she realized she still had the open photo album in her hand. She held up the album to the Beach Walk's dim streetlights. It was a picture of her and Angela — a newer photo, one taken at Devin's graduation from dental hygienist school the previous spring. Devin was in her graduation robes and Angela was wearing a pretty blue dress. She looked more like a young woman than a high school student.

Devin shrugged, closed the photo album, and put it in her bag.

"Give me your blood!" The voice echoed menacingly from the shadows between two small buildings on the Beach Walk. Devin stared into the darkness, trying to see who was threatening her. Two yellow, almond-shaped eyes stared back at her. Then a tall, dark figure flew out from the shadows.

Devin screamed as the dark figure wrapped her in his embrace. She felt wet, cold teeth sink into her throat.

CHAPTER SIX
WEDNESDAY MORNING, 12:45 A.M.

The cat followed me down the steep stairs and, nearly throwing me headlong, exasperated me to madness. Uplifting an axe . . . I aimed a blow at the animal. . . . But this blow was arrested by the hand of my wife. Goaded by the interference, into a rage more than demonical, I withdrew from her grasp and buried the axe in her brain. She fell dead upon the spot, without a groan.

A shiver raced down Angela's spine as a rush of cold night air brushed against her face. Then she heard the front door slam. She jumped from the couch, her notebook and a copy of *The Complete Tales of Edgar Allan Poe* hitting the carpet. She reached the doorway of the family room just as a dark figure ran past.

It was Devin, rushing up the stairs.

Angela sighed. "What's wrong with you?" she asked. "Can't you at least say hello or good night?"

Devin stopped halfway up the stairs. She turned. Her lips were pursed and her brow was furrowed.

"Hello and good night." She started back up the stairs again.

"Hey! What's up?" Angela started after her sister.

Devin stopped at the top of the staircase. Angela could see her sister take a deep breath. Then her shoulders slumped.

Devin turned. "I'm sorry, Angel Girl. I'm just tired and upset."

Angel Girl. Only Devin called her that. In turn, Angela called Devin "Devil Girl." They were a few years apart in age and as different as night and day, but they had always been close, especially since Devin's return three years earlier. In fact, until Devin had dyed her blond hair black, people had thought they were twins.

Devin sat down at the top of the stairs. Angela leaned on the railing just beneath her.

"You're home early." Angela looked at her watch. "Sunrise isn't for another five and a half hours."

"Yeah." Devin looked at her fingernails: One was broken and the others had the black paint chipping off them. "You know: Slice is a real jerk."

"That's old news, Dev."

"I was a few minutes late meeting him at the club, and he tries to teach me a lesson by jumping at me in the dark and biting my neck."

"What did you do?"

"I hit him with my purse. Knocked him on his butt."

Angela toed the purse sitting on the stairs. "That thing could be classified as a lethal weapon."

"And he was wearing those creepy yellow contact lenses. That'll be the last time Slice tries to scare me."

"What's his problem?"

"I don't know. Scaring me is his idea of a good time. I'm getting kind of sick of it, frankly." Devin looked up from her fingernails. "Say, what are you doing up so late?"

"Had to finish a report on Poe for Ms. Bashara."

Devin laughed. "I remember Ms. Bashara in junior English. 'The Black Cat'?"

"Yeah."

"Thought so. I think if she could, Ms. Bashara would marry Edgar Allan Poe."

Without missing a beat, Angela replied, "They're both the same age."

The sisters looked at each other and laughed. Devin stood.

"I'm going to bed. Don't stay up too late." Devin turned toward her room.

"I think I'll turn in, too. You scared the desire to study right out of me. Oh, yeah. Mom and Dad left this afternoon for New Orleans."

"I thought they weren't going until tomorrow."

"Mom said they wanted to get to the antiques show a day early to try to find some bargains before they're all gone. You're in charge of the fish and the cat."

"And what are you in charge of?"

"You. Mom says she wants me to make sure you're home every night. At least before the break of dawn."

Devin stuck her tongue out at her younger sister, laughed, and then disappeared into her bedroom.

Angela headed back downstairs, picked up her books, and shoved them into her backpack. Just as she was turning out the lights, the phone rang. Angela started, feeling her heart pound hard against her chest. Who would be calling this time of night?

The phone rang again as she reached for it. Whoever it was, she was going to tell them a thing or two. She picked up the phone, about to yell at the caller, when she heard Devin's voice. She was going to replace the phone, but the deep voice speaking to her sister was one she did not recognize. Angela had never listened in on one of her sister's telephone conversations, but a sudden curiosity overcame her. She held her breath as she covered the mouthpiece with her free hand and pressed the phone to her ear.

". . . and I hope you don't mind me calling you so late," the voice was saying.

"No, Abel," Devin said. "It's okay. I'm usually not home this early."

Who was Abel?

"I decided to check out that club you were talking about. The Umbra Club."

"Yes," Devin said. "I like the name."

You would, Angela thought. *The Umbra Club. Umbra: synonym for shadows.*

"When I didn't find you there, I got worried. You looked upset when you left the clinic."

"I was worried about you, Abel. What happened? You looked like you were having a seizure."

"Just exhaustion. That's all. I appreciate your concern. That's very thoughtful of you."

There was a long pause. Angela had to take a breath. She held the phone away from her, took a deep breath, and quickly returned the phone to her ear.

". . . wondering if you're not doing anything, maybe you'd like to go to the movies and maybe dinner," Abel was saying. "We're both off tomorrow."

"Sure," Devin said, a lilt in her voice. "Sounds like fun. All Slice wants to do is hang out at the club with his friends."

"Well, this is just a friendly get-together. My way of saying thanks for caring. I don't want to come between you and Slice."

"Believe me, Abel: I have plenty of reasons for breaking it off with Slice that don't involve you."

"Great. Pick you up at eight?"

"Sure."

"Good night, Devin."

"Good night, Abel."

"Good night, Angela," Abel said with a laugh, then hung up.

Angela gasped and slammed the phone down. She started up the stairs. Devin met her at the top.

"Mom's edict to keep an eye on me doesn't include listening to my private phone conversations." Devin stood with arms crossed.

"I'm sorry," Angela said as she reached the top of the stairs. "I really didn't mean to. But, when I heard that voice, I couldn't help it. Who is Abel?"

Devin stared at her sister for a few moments. Then she smiled. "I don't forgive you, but you're right about his voice. There's something hypnotic about it. That's Dr. Dunn."

"Your boss at the dental clinic? I thought he was an old man."

Devin laughed. "He's only twenty-three."

"How can he be a dentist so young?"

"Child genius. But he didn't want to be a doctor. He told me he always had a fascination for healthy teeth and gums."

"Sounds like a nerdy ad writer for a toothpaste company. Pretty weird, if you ask me."

They reached the doors to their respective rooms, which were across the hall from each other.

"He's a hunk, and I didn't ask you."

"What about Slice?"

"He's gone for the next week. Besides, I was thinking of dumping him. Mom and Dad would kill me if they found out I was seeing him again."

Angela yawned. "Well, six-thirty comes early. Good night."

"Night, Angela."

Angela entered her room and shut the door. Something cold brushed against her face. Something cold and fleshy, like a hand. Then for a brief, breath-catching moment, she thought she saw two yellow, almond-shaped eyes floating just in front of her, staring into her soul.

CHAPTER SEVEN
WEDNESDAY EVENING

James Hetfield's rough voice and the driving
strains of Metallica's guitars blared through the
speakers of Nina's Camaro convertible. "Enter
Sandman" was one of Nina's favorite songs.

"Yeah!" Nina yelled above the blare of the heavy
metal song and the roar of the rushing wind. She
bobbed her head back and forth in rhythm to the
driving music.

"Settle down, girl," Angela said with a laugh.
"Someone's going to think this is your first time out
in public."

"Hey! It's Wednesday night. We're out of school
for the next four days. I'm gonna get wild for a
change!" Nina yelled.

"Just make sure your driving isn't wild," Angela
yelled back.

"No problem!" Nina checked her speedometer.
The music may have been hard and fast, but her
driving was not. Playing her music loud was one

thing; reckless driving was quite another. Nina was proud of her new Camaro convertible and didn't want it taken away because she was acting foolishly behind the wheel. And she would never do anything to put one of her passengers in danger. Especially a close friend like Angela.

"I'm thirsty," Angela shouted.

"Next stop: Atomic Drive-in." Nina turned the car onto Ocean Lane. The bright neon sign advertising the Atomic Drive-in beckoned from a half mile away. A few moments later, they were parked in an empty slot.

The Atomic Drive-in had been a popular hangout for San Tomas Inlet teenagers for over forty years. It had retained its 1960s neon sign with a rocket blasting off into space. A roly-poly space man in a silver suit and bulbous space helmet hung onto one of the rocket's fins. In his free hand, he held a tray with an Atomic burger, Atomic fries, and a large Atomic drink. More popular fast-food restaurants had opened along the main drag of San Tomas Inlet, but none held the allure of the Atomic Drive-in. Even the speakers seemed to be the originals from forty years ago.

"What?" Nina shouted.

A garbled, metallic voice shouted back at her.

"This might help," Angela said, reaching over to shut off the CD player.

"I WANT AN ATOMIC BURGER AND A DIET COKE!" Nina yelled. Then she realized she was screaming when it wasn't necessary for her to do so. Patrons in other cars were laughing. Nina sank into her seat.

"There's no need to yell, miss," the metallic voice replied. "Is that all?"

Nina looked at Angela.

"Just an Atomic Float," Angela said.

Nina turned to the speaker. "One Atomic Float."

"That'll be $9.23. Thank you." The speaker popped, gurgled, and was silent.

"He better thank me with the prices they're charging," Nina said, digging into her pocket for the money. "I'll be glad when the tourist season is completely over and the prices go back to normal. I hope that beef is chopped sirloin and not mashed-up soy."

Angela laughed. "I told you to eat at home."

"I can't believe you want a root beer float. Thought you were trying to be healthy."

"A girl just wants to have fun." Angela sat back in her seat.

"When are the folks coming home?"

"Sunday evening sometime. Maybe Monday. Mom called and said they had arrived but that there was more to look at than they'd thought. She was happy when I told her you were staying the weekend."

Nina turned on the CD player, but kept it just

low enough to be audible. "Where's Ms. Goth? I thought you were in charge of her."

"Devin is old enough to take care of herself. I wish Mom and Dad would realize that. She's really changed."

"Yeah. She's using midnight-death nail polish instead of just plain old black."

"No, she really has changed. She loves her job, and she's paying Mom and Dad back all the money they sent her."

"Wait 'til they find out she's seeing Slice again. I don't know what she ever saw in that guy. I mean, who would name himself after a lemon-lime soft drink?"

Angela laughed. "I think he meant it to sound menacing. He probably never thought about the soft drink. Besides, I think that might be over. She's actually on a date with one of the dentists from the clinic right now."

"Really? Who?"

"Dr. Dunn. He's new. Only been there a month. Devin likes him, I think."

"I don't think your mom and dad are going to like her dating an older man."

"He's not old —" Devin began.

"Here you go, ladies," interrupted a young girl carrying a large tray. She was wearing a silver outfit much like the neon spaceman, and the hat on her head was round and silver. "One Atomic burger, one Atomic large Diet Coke, and one Atomic Float. That'll be $9.23."

"Super," Nina said with a grimace. She handed the girl a wad of ten one-dollar bills. "Keep the change."

The girl counted the bills, smiled sarcastically, and said, "Thanks."

Nina handed the float to Angela.

"HEY! We're just in time for dinner!" yelled Captain Bob, out of nowhere. He skated up to the passenger side of the car.

Both Angela and Nina started. Nina had been passing Angela the float when Bob had startled them. The girls' sudden motion tipped the cup, and ice cream oozed all over Angela's arm.

"Watch it!" Nina grabbed a napkin and wrapped it around Angela's hand and wrist. "Smooth move, Captain Boob!" She sighed. "You almost got this all over my new car."

"Sorry," Captain Bob said, trying his best to look apologetic.

As she mopped up the float, Nina felt a heavy hand fall on her shoulder. She threw her arms up in the air, knocking the cup from Angela's hand. Nina and Angela watched in horror as the cup sailed into the air as if in slow motion. Nina imagined its contents spilling over the white leather interior of her new Camaro.

"Gotcha!" Bob cried, catching the cup on its way down. "Never fear, Captain Bob is here."

"Sorry," came a voice from behind Nina.

Nina turned. It was Joe. "You frightened ten years off my life, Joe!"

"I didn't mean to," Joe said, looking down at the pavement.

"Hey, no harm, no foul. You gonna drink this?" Bob asked. He wiped the root beer that had coated his hands onto the lip of the cup, the excess dripping inside.

"Not now," said Angela. Bob eagerly took a swig.

"What are you two doing here, anyway?" Nina said.

"Ooking for you," Bob said as he drank.

"I called your house," Joe said. "Your mom said you and Angela were out driving around. Captain Bob suggested we put on our skates and look for you."

"Why?" Nina said.

"We need your help," Bob said, finishing the last of the float. He smacked his lips.

Nina looked at the freshman. Bob had a big smile on his face and a dull brown root beer mustache on his upper lip. *How did I ever get mixed up with these boys?* she asked herself, not for the first time. She couldn't help liking them, but sometimes they drove her nuts.

"We've been talking to Detective Turner," Joe began. "About the murders. We've learned something that involves Angela."

Angela turned toward him. "What do you mean?"

Joe leaned into the car, close to Nina. "Detective Turner doesn't believe that a large animal is running around killing people," he said. "He thinks some weird blood cult is operating in or around San Tomas. He's worked up a profile of the type of people who might be in this cult: social outcasts, loners, people with an unnatural interest in death and the occult; people who'd rather be up all night and sleep all day. That's when I thought of you."

Angela's eyes widened in understanding and anger. "You think my sister is one of those kind of people because of the way she dresses?"

Joe looked puzzled at Angela's outburst. "No. No. Not at all," he protested.

"Then what do you mean?" Angela's eyes were slits of anger.

"I — well — I — just —"

"He just meant that you might know someone like that," Bob chimed in. "Like Slice."

Angela turned to Bob, focusing her angry eyes on him.

"Whoa," Bob said, taking a step backward.

"Yeah," Joe said. "We didn't tell Detective Turner. Not yet."

"Tell him what?" Angela said slowly.

"Well," Joe said slowly. "What we found out."

"And what was that?" Angela said. She stared straight ahead into the dash of the car.

"What are you two boys up to?" Nina demanded.

"We checked the dates of the attacks against the dates when Slice claimed he was out of town," Bob said. "Including the attack on Todd."

"They all match," Joe added.

"What matches?" Nina said.

"The dates of the attacks and the dates when Slice was on the road," Joe said. "We found Solid Flesh's tour schedule on the band's Web site. They match. And the places where the bodies were found match the routes Slice and his band would have taken to get to their gigs. We think Slice and his crew stole the boat and attacked Todd and his dad."

"You're telling me," Angela began, "that my sister is dating a bloodsucking cult leader?"

Bob and Joe looked at each other. Then Bob said, "Well, yeah."

Angela reached out and pushed Bob. Caught unaware, Bob rolled backward on his in-line skates and hit the car next to Nina's.

"Hey!" yelled a large teenager from the other car. He pushed Bob away from his car. His shove was more forceful than Angela's, and Bob lost his balance, falling forward. He reached out for anything to help him catch his balance, but grabbed only empty air. His knees hit the ground with a thud.

"Yeow," Bob said, grimacing. "That's gonna leave a scar."

"I'm sorry, Angela," Joe said. "We wouldn't have

said anything, but we found this at Slice's apartment." He pulled a thin, well-worn paperback book from his hip pocket.

"You broke into someone's apartment?" Nina said incredulously.

"Well, no," Bob said, grunting as he stood. "One of his roommates let us in. We told him Slice had forgotten his guitar picks, and he let us search Slice's room."

Joe held the book out toward Nina and Angela. Angela continued to stare straight ahead, but Nina could read the cover clearly.

The cover was bloodred. In large, black Gothic letters with gold trim was written: *The Legend of the Vampire.*

CHAPTER EIGHT
THURSDAY MORNING

"You know, I will never figure out why that coyote just doesn't catch and eat that Road Runner," Nina said. She sat cross-legged on the floor, a bowl of cereal in her hand. She had one eye on the TV.

"It's only a cartoon," Angela said.

"I know it's only a cartoon, but it's silly. Coyotes are smart. Roadrunners are just birds."

"Then watch something else."

Nina turned to her friend. Angela sat with her legs up, her head resting to one side. Her cereal and toast were untouched.

"You're not still thinking about what those two maniacs said, are you?" Nina said.

"Pretty weird," Angela replied.

"If you mean Joe and Bob, then you're right."

"Yeah, them too." Angela sighed. "Does look pretty strange, though. Slice and his band being out of town and in the area where the victims were found. They were right about the night Todd was attacked, too. Slice was supposed to have been playing in a little club about five miles from where Todd and his father were fishing."

"Just coincidence," Nina said.

"I don't know. Did you read any of that book, *The Legend of the Vampire?*"

"No. It's probably just a novel or stories about vampires."

"I read it."

"When?"

"Last night. I couldn't sleep. Joe gave it to me before he and Bob left. It's pretty spooky. It's not a novel. It's actually a book about vampire worshiping, how to become a vampire, rituals, stuff like that."

"Sounds crazy to me," Nina said, shrugging.

Angela sighed. "There's something I haven't told you."

"What?"

"Devin told me that Slice tried to attack her the other night. Tried to bite her throat."

"He's just a jerk."

"I also thought I saw him standing in my room."

"What?"

"When I was going to bed that same night. I closed my door and felt a hand brush across my face. Then I saw two glowing yellow eyes. It looked like Slice. I turned on the light, but he had disappeared."

"You were probably just tired. Having a waking dream."

"I don't know." Angela looked at her friend sadly. "Ever since Todd was attacked and almost killed" — Angela fought back tears — "I don't know what to believe. He insists a giant wolf attacked him. A wolf that can walk on two legs like a man."

"Todd was delirious."

"I visited him yesterday afternoon."

"Todd? Is he awake yet?"

"Yes, but only for short periods of time." Angela's lower lip quivered. "He kept saying he should have stayed and helped his dad, that he feels like a coward. I tried to talk to him, to tell him that his dad would be okay, that he wasn't a coward, but the nurse told me I had to leave."

Nina was about to reply when a noise behind them startled both girls.

"Morning, ladies." Devin walked slowly into the room. She was dressed in black cotton pajamas. Her hair was mussed and stood out in all directions. She wasn't wearing any eyeliner or eye shadow, and she looked ghostly.

"I see the de-tanning sessions are working," Nina said, taking a bite of toast.

"What?" Devin asked sleepily, sinking into an oversized armchair.

"De-tanning sessions. You know, it's the opposite of a tanning salon. They wrap you from head to foot in a towel and stick you in a closet for an hour so you'll get pale. You're getting your money's worth."

"Oh," Devin responded, without enthusiasm. "I get it. You're pretty funny in the morning. Too bad there's not much call for early morning comedians."

"Speaking of early mornings, what are you doing up?" Angela asked.

"I haven't been to bed yet. I heard the TV and came down to observe the habits of day dwellers."

"How'd the date with Dr. Bicuspid go?" Nina inquired.

"What?"

"Your date with Abel," Angela explained.

"Oh. Fine. He's a nice guy." Devin's eyes were closed. She appeared to be talking in her sleep. "Good to meet a nice guy for a change. He's pretty funny, too. He's got an attractive smile."

"Be a little ironic if he had a terrible smile," Nina said. "I mean, what with him being a dentist, you'd hope he'd have a pretty smile with pearly white teeth and healthy pink gums."

"Um. Yes," Devin said.

"That's pretty," Angela said, noticing a choker around Devin's neck. It was black satin with a silver dragon clasped in the middle. "When did you get that?"

Angela looked more closely. "Unusual, too. I don't think I've ever seen a dragon designed like this one." She stared at it. The dragon twisted and turned like a snake, with wings like a large bat, fire-red eyes, and sharp teeth. She reached out to touch it.

Suddenly, Devin sat up. She grabbed Angela's hand and twisted her sister's arm away. "Don't touch it! It's mine! He gave it to me!" She let go and fell back into the large chair, sinking into the cushions. She closed her eyes and whispered, "It's mine. He gave it to me."

A chill swept through the room. Nina stared at the sleeping Devin and her sister, Angela, who was rubbing her sore wrist.

LATER THAT NIGHT

"I thought you'd be out cruising again tonight," Bob said with a smile as Angela walked up to the counter of the Beach Burger, a local beachfront hamburger shack.

"I called in sick. The cruisers will just have to do without me for a night," Angela answered, smiling back at him. "I wanted to talk to you about what you and Joe said last night."

Bob quickly hopped up, slid over the counter, and stood next to a surprised Angela. "Take over, Hubert," he instructed a pimply faced teenager who was sweeping up behind the counter. "Let's sit over here." Bob motioned to a booth in the corner.

"Won't you get in trouble?"

"Nah. My mom manages this place. She wants me to learn the value of hard work and responsibility, so she sticks me down here some nights."

"You learning anything?" Angela asked. They slid into the booth.

"Sure. I don't like hard work or responsibility."

Angela smiled.

"You want something to drink? I'm buying." Bob started to stand up.

"No. Besides, you have to pay for it, don't you?"

Bob sat down and leaned across the table. He whispered, "I'm supposed to, part of the responsibility thing. It's supposed to come out of my salary. But it doesn't. Unless Hubert over there is looking" — he pointed his thumb at the gangly teen, who was wiping the counter and eyeing them suspiciously — "and rats on me to my mom. I'd fire him if she'd let me."

"Then you'd have to do all the work yourself."

Bob sat back against the booth's seat. "Hey. Yeah. You're right. You're pretty smart."

Angela smiled again. "About what you said last night. The vampire cult. You don't really think there is such a thing, do you?"

Bob took off his Beach Burger cap and put on his yacht captain's hat, which he kept folded in half in his hip pocket.

"That's better. Now I feel like a new man." He leaned forward, clasping his hands. "There are more things in heaven and earth than are dreamt of in our philosophies, Angela."

Angela laughed. "I studied *Hamlet,* Bob. I'm not

here for a Shakespeare lesson. I just want to know if you really believe all that vampire stuff."

Captain Bob leaned back again. "I guess. Sounds logical to me."

"I mean, vampires? Are there really people out there who believe they're vampires?"

"Apparently," Bob said. "I'd say your sister's friend Slice thinks he's one."

"I don't know. I always thought vampires and werewolves and monsters were just in books and the movies."

"Well, this isn't a movie or a book. This is real life, and it appears we have a vampire cult right here in San Tomas."

Angela shook her head. "I don't know."

A shadow fell over them. "Don't know what?" asked a gruff voice.

Bob looked up. "Slice!"

"Slice?" Angela said in surprise. "Wh-what are you doing here? I thought you and your band —"

"Never mind that." Slice placed his hands on the table and leaned toward Angela. "Where's Devin? I called your house, and she's not there."

"She's at work," Angela answered, her lip trembling.

"I walked down to that butcher's clinic, and she ain't there neither."

"You know," Bob began, "the use of the double negative in English is actually —"

Slice pulled Bob out of the booth and onto his feet. Slice was thin, pale, and looked sickly, but he possessed a hidden strength that surprised Bob. A silver pentagram dangled from one of his ears.

"Look, slime worm, I'm not talking to you. When I'm talking to you, I'll say 'Hey, slime worm.' Get it?"

Bob stared into Slice's eyes. "You know," he began, "those yellow contacts make you look like a traffic light stuck on yield."

Slice let go of Bob, and he fell to the floor, his sore knees buckling under him.

"I don't know where Devin is, Slice," Angela said. "She's an adult. She can do what she wants."

"What's that supposed to mean?"

"It means that I don't baby-sit my sister. I don't know where she is."

"Hey, Slice," someone yelled from the doorway. A young man ran up to Slice. He looked at Bob, a hint of recognition coming over him. "Hey, I know you. Slice, this is the dude who came to the apartment looking for your picks last night."

"Hey," Bob said with a salute to the roommate.

Slice turned to Bob again. "What were you doing in my apartment, you little runt?"

"Looking for CDs of your band. Can't find them in stores anywhere, so I thought maybe you had a few hundred lying around your apartment."

Slice grabbed Bob again. "I'm going to rip your

throat out." Slice opened his mouth to reveal teeth that came to razor-sharp points.

"Dude, I'd hate to have your orthodontist's bill," Bob said, shaking his head.

"Put him down," came a deep voice.

Slice turned slowly. Standing in the doorway of the Beach Burger was a tall dark man dressed in a dark shirt and black Levi's. His black hair flowed down to his shoulders, and his deep brown eyes pierced through Slice's yellow contacts.

Standing next to the tall dark man, her arm draped in his, was Devin.

Slice shoved Bob. He hit the floor again. "Why am I always the guy who ends up on the floor?" Bob asked, grimacing.

"That's what I came in to tell you," said the roommate. "I saw 'em coming up the boardwalk."

Slice walked over to the man and Devin. He grabbed Devin's free arm.

"C'mon, Devin. We gotta go."

Devin didn't move.

"I said, C'mon!"

"She's with me, friend," the man said.

"I'm not your friend," Slice said, pointing a finger in the man's face. "Just who do you think you are?"

"This is Dr. Dunn," Devin answered.

Slice looked at Devin. "The dentist? This is the guy you work for? You're going out with a *dentist?*"

"We just came in to get a bite to eat, Slice," Abel said. "That's all. Devin wasn't feeling well at work, so we closed up, and I brought her down here to eat something. Anything else you think might be going on is just a figment of your weak imagination."

"A figment of my imagination?"

"Actually, he said *weak* imagination," Bob put in.

Slice turned to Bob. "I'll take care of you later." Then he turned back to Devin and grabbed her arm again.

Just as quickly, Abel smacked Slice's arm away and grabbed the thin man by his T-shirt. "Look, friend: All we want is a little food and peace and quiet. Now, Devin will call you later. All right?"

Slice looked around for help. His roommate backed away, shaking his head. "All right," Slice finally gurgled.

Abel let go of Slice, and he stumbled to the floor. His roommate helped him to his feet.

Slice started toward the door, but turned back for one parting shot. "You all have made a big mistake. I'd sleep with one eye open tonight, *friends*." Then he was gone.

"Hey, that was pretty cool," Bob said. "You can come out now, Hubert." He leaned over the counter to find the teenager huddled in one of the empty cubbyholes. "Danger has passed. You have a customer.

"Order anything you want," Bob told Abel and

Devin. "On the house. Hey, you want anything, Angela?" Bob looked past Abel and Devin toward the booth. Angela was gone. He glanced at the front door just in time to see it close.

Hubert cleared his throat and said in a dull voice, "Would you like our special? Tonight's special is the Beach Burger combo: half-pound hamburger, jumbo fries, giant drink of your choice, and a free Beach Burger place mat with puzzles for your entertainment."

"Just take their order," Bob said to Hubert.

"Just a couple of hamburgers, fries, and Diet Cokes, please," Abel said.

"And how would you like those burgers cooked, sir?" Hubert said as he slowly wrote the order.

"Rare."

"Want to hear the 'moo,' huh?" Bob said with a smile.

Abel turned to Bob, returning the smile. "Something like that."

Bob hobbled around the counter and made their drinks. "Have a seat. I'll bring these out to you."

Bob brought the drinks and joined the pair at a table. "So, you're the new dentist?"

"Yes. Been here about a month."

"I'd like to know what vitamins you're taking."

"What?"

"Well, you look so young."

"I'm only twenty-three."

"Twenty-three? I've never heard of a twenty-three-year-old dentist. What did you do, buy your dentist's license over the Internet?" Bob said with a laugh.

"No. I was considered a child prodigy. I finished high school by the time I was twelve years old and went to college. Then I started medical school, but I got bored and decided to go into dentistry."

"Dentistry? Why? I always thought doctors did more exciting work."

"Less blood," Abel said with a smile. "I can't stand the sight of too much blood. Makes me queasy."

"Oh," Bob said as though he understood, but he didn't. "Tell me, what's it like to be a child genius?"

"I expect it's the same as being of average intelligence," Abel replied, grinning. "Only less confusing."

Bob laughed slowly. "You worried about Slice?" he asked, changing the subject.

"No," was all Abel said.

"You know he's a vampire?"

"Really?" Abel asked, raising an eyebrow.

"Here you go, folks." Hubert put a tray on the table.

"Put it on my tab," Bob said.

"You don't have a tab," Hubert said, walking away.

Bob frowned. "Lousy service around here." He took the food baskets from the tray and set them in front of Abel and Devin. "You don't seem surprised."

"About what?" Abel took a big bite of hamburger. Juice squirted from the edge of the hamburger and dripped onto the table.

"Oh, garçon," Bob said, waving at Hubert. "Spill on table three." He turned back to Abel. "You don't seem surprised that Slice is a vampire."

Abel wiped his lips with a napkin. "Hey, it's the millennium. Anything's possible. I'm more disappointed that we don't have flying cars in the twenty-first century."

Bob laughed. Abel was pretty cool for an adult. "Yeah, and instant learning helmets so we don't have to go to school." Bob grabbed a french fry from Devin's basket and gobbled it down. "Seriously, Slice is a vampire, or at least he thinks he is. I found a book called *The Legend of the Vampire* at his apartment. And tonight I got an up-close-and-personal look at his teeth." Bob leaned closer. "He's had them filed down to points."

"Ouch. I'd hate to have his orthodontist's bill," Abel said, taking another bite of his burger.

"Hey! That's what I said. Great minds think alike, huh?"

"Yeah, I suppose so." Abel turned to Devin. "What's wrong? You're so quiet, and you're not eating."

Devin moaned softly. "I'm not feeling well, Abel. Please take me home. I think I'm gonna be sick."

"Sure," Abel said. "I'm sorry. I was just talking to our new friend here."

Bob smiled. "Want a doggy bag for that?" he said, pointing to the food.

"No, thank you." Abel stood and then helped Devin get up. "Come on, you look terrible."

"Thank you, Abel," Devin whispered.

Bob followed as they headed to the door. "I'll walk you to your car."

"That's okay," Abel said.

"Hey, Hubert," Bob began, ignoring Abel. "I'll be back in a minute. Hold down the fort."

Hubert made a grunting noise in reply.

As they headed toward the car, Bob asked, "So, what made you move to San Tomas Inlet? We're not exactly the hub of Florida."

"It was the only place with a night dental clinic."

"Well, you picked a good time to move here."

"Why do you say that?" Abel said.

"Seems we have a vampire cult operating here."

"So Slice is not only a vampire, he's the leader of a vampire cult?"

"Yeah."

They walked down the boardwalk. Devin's arm was crooked through Abel's for support.

"You're just kidding, right?" Abel said with a chuckle.

"No, really. Devin's boyfriend is a vampire. My friend Joe and I found that book at his apartment. Plus he's been conveniently out of town during each of the murders."

"Sounds pretty far-fetched," Abel replied. "I always thought vampires were myths."

"Maybe. Maybe not. All I know is that Detective Turner says they've called in an FBI profiler."

"An FBI profiler?"

"Yeah, so they can write up a behavioral profile of the cult members. Joe and I are helping them."

"It seems you and your friend are pretty important around here."

Bob swaggered as he walked.

They finally reached the car. Abel gently helped Devin inside.

"Drive safely," Bob told them as Abel climbed into the driver's side.

"Thanks. I will. Keep me informed about those vampires." Abel smiled, started the car, and sped away.

Bob walked back to the Beach Burger. Hubert had already turned the OPEN sign to CLOSED. Bob told him he could go home. The gangly teen didn't hesitate.

Bob locked up and he spent the next half an hour sweeping and cleaning the Beach Burger. He turned off the restaurant's neon sign as the restaurant's clock struck midnight. He put on his leather jacket and left the Beach Burger.

I wonder what happened to Angela, he thought as he hopped on his moped. He revved up the bike's small engine, put on his helmet, and took off toward home. He couldn't wait until he was old enough to own a real motorcycle. He imagined himself driving down I-95 with a gorgeous blonde on the back.

He was particularly proud of his leather jacket. He had bought it with some of the money he had earned during his internship at Universal Studios. Joe had bought an identical one, and both had had "Born to Raze Hell" embroidered on the back. Nina thought the slogan was a little silly, but they didn't care. It was funny, and it fit in with their interest in the paranormal.

The night was cool. Dark clouds moved slowly across the sky. Bob glanced up once to catch a glimpse of the full moon as it peeked from behind a cloud. Fall was settling upon San Tomas Inlet. Daylight was growing shorter and the nights were growing longer. Unlike southern Florida, the north-central coast didn't stay warm all year like the resorts to the south. The summer months were perfect for summer beach bums, but as autumn and winter came on, the temperature dropped into the chilly zone.

He twisted the right handle grip. The moped sputtered and sped up a little. Bob felt a cool breeze rush up his right arm. Then he felt a tickle. He took his left hand from the brake handle and steadily scratched his right arm through the leather jacket. The tickling stopped.

A few seconds later, the tickling returned, and

this time it seemed to run up and down his arm. He scratched the length of his arm. The tickling didn't stop. Bob scratched harder.

Something pierced his arm. "Ow!" he screamed. The sting was so sudden and painful that Bob released the bike's handlebars. The moped's front wheel swerved back and forth. Bob quickly grabbed the handlebars and steadied the moped on the road.

Then he felt the same pain in his left arm. And not just in one spot: Up and down his arms, the piercing continued, like someone sticking dozens of needles into both his arms. He found it hard to hold on to the bike. His arms began to shake, and the front wheel of the moped wobbled. He tried to press the hand brake, but found he had no strength in his left arm. The moped seemed to speed up all on its own.

Tears came to Bob's eyes as the pain intensified. His arms felt as though they were on fire. Bob tried to squeeze the brake but again found that he had no strength to stop the bike. He felt as though some force were behind him, pushing the bike to go faster and faster. The front wheel wobbled farther to the left and then back to the right, and the whole bike shook. Bob knew that at this speed, he would be badly injured if he hit the pavement. With what strength he could muster, he guided the moped to the edge of the road.

The front wheel of the moped hit the sand that

kissed up to the asphalt road, and the bike stopped immediately. Bob fell onto the sand, rolling for several yards. The moped's engine whined loudly and the back wheel spun wildly.

Bob rolled onto his knees and quickly pulled off his leather jacket, throwing it away from him. He cried out when he saw dozens of large objects on his arms. They were the size of silver dollars — oval-shaped, with fat bodies, six small legs, and tiny heads that ended in a point. They nearly covered his arms. Bob hated bugs, but he hated these bugs most of all. They were giant ticks.

Bob tried brushing them off, but some had already embedded their heads into his flesh. Their bodies pulsated as they drank his blood.

Bob grabbed one, twisted the body, and pulled it from his arm. He heard a snap and realized the tick's head was still in his arm. A drop of blood squirted from the tick's body. His blood.

He began pulling at the ticks' bodies one by one. Each time he pulled one from his arm, he heard a sickening snap and then saw blood squirt from a headless body. He tossed the bodies away from him, but the decapitated ticks just started scrambling toward him, crawling up his legs toward his arms again.

In desperation, Bob grabbed the headless bodies and began squeezing them with his thumb and forefinger until their bodies popped, bug juice and blood squirting his arms and face. He jumped to his feet and stomped on the headless bodies trying to reach him. He clawed at the remaining ticks that were sucking the lifeblood out of him.

Suddenly, Bob felt a tickle at his throat, then a sharp, piercing pain. He reached up and felt a tick boring into his neck, just above the artery.

He pulled the tick from his throat. Pain shot from his neck. Then he remembered something from biology class — something he hoped would save his life.

Bob staggered to the downed moped. The engine had died and the bike lay still. He fell to his knees and twisted the cap to the small gas tank. He cupped his hands under the gasoline as it poured from the tank and splashed it on his arms. Bob screamed as the gasoline stung where the bodiless heads of the ticks were still trying to bore deeper into his flesh. The ticks writhed in pain and began to pull out of his arms.

Bob splashed more gasoline on his arms and neck. His eyes teared up as the fumes hit his eyes and throat. He could barely see or breathe. He felt like he was going to throw up.

Bob stood and began stomping the ticks as they fell from his arms. His head felt as though it would explode. Darkness began to cover him.

Then he fell to the ground and lay still.

CHAPTER NINE
LATE THURSDAY EVENING

"Are you sure you're going to be okay?" Abel asked as he and Devin reached the front door of her house.

"Yes, thank you," she replied in a whisper. "I'll be fine."

"Maybe you ought to take tomorrow off. I'll call Sylvia to take your place."

"I need the money."

"You need the rest." He held her by the shoulders, then leaned forward and kissed her on the forehead. "Now to sleep; perchance to dream."

Devin tried to smile. Something about Abel had a calming effect on her. Despite her fatigue and illness, she felt safe in his embrace. In a flash, she decided that Slice was history and Abel was the new sheriff in town. "I don't think you have the quote right."

Abel laughed. "It's the thought that counts. Good night." He took her keys from her hand, unlocked the door, opened it, and gently pushed her inside.

"Stay home tomorrow, rest, and I'll call you after work to check up on you."

"Good night, sweet prince."

"Now *you're* mixing up quotes."

Devin smiled and closed the door. She leaned against the door and listened as Abel walked away. The sickness within her receded a little. She turned to head upstairs to bed.

A cold hand grabbed her by the throat.

"Finally made it home, my dear?"

"What are you doing here, Slice?" Devin tried to pull away from Slice's icy grip.

"Waiting for the love of my life to get home."

"How did you get in here?"

"We have our ways of entering through locked doors and windows."

"We?"

"Vampires!" Slice leaned forward. In the dim light, Devin could see Slice's open mouth and pointed teeth. "It is time for you to join us." Hot breath hit her throat.

A deep voice resonated in the entryway. "Little boys shouldn't play grown-up games."

Devin saw a dark shadow behind Slice. It reached out and grabbed him by the throat. Slice grunted and loosened his grip on Devin. She slid out from Slice's grip and ran to stand near Abel.

"I'm sorry to interfere with you and your boyfriend, but he just doesn't know how to treat a lady."

"Let — go — of — me," Slice said, his voice high-pitched and breathless.

Abel let go. Slice gasped for air.

"You're a dead man," Slice said, coughing.

Abel smiled. "Time to say good-bye." He reached behind Slice and opened the door.

Slice looked at Devin and then at Abel. "This ain't over."

Abel shoved Slice out the door. Slice stumbled and fell on the sidewalk. "It is for tonight, chump." Abel closed the door firmly.

"Thank you," said Devin, smiling weakly.

"I'll wait until you're up the stairs, and then I'll make sure lover boy is gone for good."

Devin smiled. "Thank you," she whispered again. She started slowly up the stairs, taking each step carefully, trying to decide whether to go to bed or invite Abel to stay and talk. She reached the top and turned around.

She gasped. Abel was gone. He had left so quietly she hadn't heard the door open or close.

Devin sighed. Tomorrow. Tomorrow she would call Abel to invite him for a candlelight dinner after work, and then maybe a late drive along the beach.

Devin went to bed with a smile on her face. She felt a gentle calm wash over her as she slipped into sleep. But her dreams were a labyrinth of distorted and grotesque images. Flashes of red light illuminated a sky full of black clouds. The images wobbled and rolled and transformed themselves from one odd shape into another.

A dark figure walked among the hideous shapes and reached out to her. She tried to run, but her legs were heavy and her feet were welded to the ever-changing ground. The figure gripped her in a bone-chilling clutch. She tried to run, to get away. She ground her teeth. She gasped for air. And then the figure took a definite form and shape.

Slice stood before her, his bright-yellow eyes shining like two small suns, his face twisted in hate, and his mouth open wide to reveal deadly teeth. "Time now, my love. Time to join us."

Slice sunk his teeth deep into her throat.

CHAPTER TEN
EARLY FRIDAY AFTERNOON

"This is amazing," Angela said, looking up from the newspaper as Devin entered the room. "This makes two days in a row that you've made an appearance before dark." She took a bite of her muffin.

Devin threw herself into her favorite chair and curled up into a ball.

"Mom said you're to mow the lawn, and she doesn't want you to wait until midnight and bother the neighbors."

"I didn't sleep well," Devin said, her voice weak and hoarse. "I had nightmares all night."

"Mom and Dad don't get back until Sunday night," Angela said. "I don't care when you do it as long as you get it done before they get back."

Devin didn't answer. Angela glanced up from the comics section. Devin looked paler than normal. Without her dark eye shadow and eyeliner, she looked more like a porcelain doll than a Goth fan.

"You want to lie down on the couch?" Angela asked her sister.

"I think I'll go back to bed." Devin tried to stand, but fell back into the chair. "Maybe I'll just stay here." She closed her eyes.

Angela threw the paper on the floor in front of the couch. "Can I get you anything?"

"You can close the curtains. It's too bright in here."

Angela looked at Devin. Then she slowly turned her head and looked at the curtains. They were already closed. The only light in the room was the one by which Angela had been reading the newspaper.

"Where's your friend Nina?" Devin asked.

"She went to see Bob. He had an accident on the way home last night," Angela replied.

"Yes," Devin said.

"What?" Angela sat up.

Devin didn't answer.

"Are you awake?"

Devin opened her eyes. Normally, her bright-blue eyes would shine in the slightest of light. But the blue was now dull and faded.

"Devin," Angela began, "I want to talk to you about Slice."

Devin closed her eyes. "Slice," she said with a hiss.

"Bob and Joe think that Slice is mixed up with some sort of vampire cult." She reached under a pillow on the couch and brought forth a book with a red cover and black lettering with gold trim.

"They found this in Slice's apartment." She held out *The Legend of the Vampire.*

Devin opened her eyes. She smiled and then closed her eyes again. "Slice," she hissed again.

"That's why I left the Beach Burger when you and Abel came in. I can't stand Slice, and I didn't want to get in the middle of a fight." Angela stared at her sister. "I went to the hospital and spent some time with Todd."

"How is he?" Devin said.

Angela smiled, but tears welled in her eyes. "He's awake, but he's just staring at the ceiling, like he's in some sort of waking coma. I talked to him, but he didn't respond, not even when I kissed him good night."

"I'm sorry, Angela."

Angela wiped at her eyes with the back of her hand. She looked at her sister. "Devin, is Slice mixed up in anything — anything terrible?"

Devin sat still, barely breathing. "Slice. He was here when I came home. We talked. I was tired. I don't remember. I think he kissed me."

Angela threw the book on top of the newspaper. She stared at her sister. "Devin, I think the police want to question Slice and his band, especially about when they were touring in the area. Seems that Slice and his band were somewhere around when the killings took place."

Devin suddenly sat up and started coughing. The sound was hard and dry.

"Are you okay?" Angela knelt beside her sister. Devin leaned back into the big chair.

"I'm just sick," Devin said with a weak smile. "I'm okay. Really I am, Angela. I saw Slice last night. You don't have to worry about him."

Now Angela could see that Devin's skin was not just pale, it was nearly translucent. There were blue veins visible beneath her skin. She placed her palm against her sister's forehead. It was cold and clammy. No fever. Angela remembered that cold and clammy could mean heat exhaustion. But it wasn't hot enough for heat exhaustion.

Devin appeared to have fallen asleep. She breathed deeply. A glint of metal caught Angela's eye. The choker with the dragon clasp was still around Devin's neck.

She turned and quickly picked up the vampire book. She held the cover next to Devin's face. The dragon on the book's cover and the dragon on Devin's clasp were exactly the same.

Devin coughed again, but she didn't open her eyes. A small drop of blood trickled from the corner of her mouth. Angela reached over and pulled open Devin's mouth.

Angela gasped. Devin's nearly perfect teeth had a reddish hue. She must have bitten herself when she coughed. Then Angela noticed that Devin's canine teeth were longer and tapered to sharp points.

Angela reached down to examine the dragon clasp on the choker.

Devin's eyes popped open. Angela screamed as bright, luminous yellow eyes stared back at her. A guttural growl filled the room. Angela scooted backward as Devin rose from the chair. But she wasn't standing: She was floating several inches above the floor.

Angela pressed against the couch, her eyes wide, her mouth open, and her breathing short and quick.

"So, you want to know about vampires, Angela?" Devin stretched her arms out and opened her mouth.

Angela screamed as her sister fell upon her.

CHAPTER ELEVEN
LATER THAT AFTERNOON

"I think you fell asleep, hit your head on the road, and had a nightmare," Nina said. She sat in a worn recliner, flipping through a motorcycle magazine.

"I think hitting your head may have increased your IQ," Joe added with a smile. He sat on the floor because the only other piece of furniture, a couch as well-worn as the chair, was occupied by Bob.

Bob lay still with a wet washcloth over his forehead. He had a few bruises but no broken bones or other serious injuries. At least, he didn't think so.

After he'd fallen down, he'd gotten up and managed to make it to the cool seawater. He'd been splashing the dark, salty liquid over him when he suddenly realized the ticks were gone. The ride home in his wet clothes and wet jacket had chilled him. He'd shivered all through the night and had called his friends first thing in the morning, hoping to get a little sympathy. Instead, all he got was sarcasm and indifference.

"I didn't fall asleep," Bob protested. "I was wide awake and I was attacked by giant ticks."

"If you were attacked by giant ticks," Nina began, "then where are the scars?"

Bob held up his arms. There were a few scratches and bruises, but nothing to indicate that giant ticks had tried to suck the lifeblood out of him.

"What about my neck?" he asked. "Do I have any punctures on my neck?"

"Just a pimple," Joe said, grinning.

"Very funny, laughing boy." Bob rolled off the couch and stood up. He wobbled on his feet.

Joe steadied him. "I thought you said your mom told you not to get up," Joe said.

"I've got to see for myself." Bob walked down the narrow hallway into the bathroom. He looked at himself in the mirror. His face was scratched. He checked his throat. No bites or puncture marks. He checked his arms again. Still nothing to indicate that he had been attacked by giant ticks. He sighed and returned to his friends.

"Well?" Nina said.

"I'm telling you I was attacked by giant ticks."

Nina shook her head. "Look, if you were attacked by giant ticks and you killed them like you said you did, we would have found their bodies when Joe and I checked out the area on the way over."

"No dead ticks?" Bob said, flopping back down on the couch.

"No dead ticks, buddy," Joe replied.

"Curiouser and curiouser," Bob said.

"Just admit you fell asleep and wrecked your moped," Nina said sympathetically. "No one's going to think you're uncool."

"What did your mom say?" Joe said.

"She's not going to let me close the Beach Burger anymore," Bob said. "That's just fine with me." He looked at his two friends. "Thanks for coming over."

"That's okay," Joe said. "I always come running when a friend of mine wakes me at the crack of dawn screaming hysterically about being attacked by giant ticks."

"Yeah," Nina added. "And I brought something to cheer you up." She pulled a comic book from a plastic bag. "Joe says you like this stuff." She handed it to Bob.

"Wow!" Bob shouted, grabbing it. "A 1964 *Hunchback of Notre Dame* Classic Comic. This is rare." He flipped through the yellowed pages of the comic. "Thanks." He looked at Nina. "This must have cost a fortune."

Nina blushed. "I got it from Angela's parents' antique store. And you're welcome, Captain Bob."

"Speaking of which," Joe said, handing Bob the yacht captain's cap. "We found this at the beach. Figured you'd want it."

"Far out." Bob grabbed the hat, sat up, and placed it on his head. He looked at both of his friends. "I know what you're thinking, but I was attacked by giant ticks, and I think they were sent by Slice and his vampire cult."

Nina sighed. "Here we go again."

"I believe him," Joe said.

Nina frowned at Joe. "What?"

"There's something I haven't told you guys," Joe said.

"What's that?" Nina said.

Bob watched his friend. He knew Joe well enough to know when his friend was serious and when he was pulling a practical joke. He could tell Joe had something important to say, and this wasn't the time for a wisecrack.

"What is it, Joe?" Bob said.

"Remember the night of the storm, when we were going to watch those horror movies on the special projector?"

"I remember that I'm still paying for my mom's carpet," Nina said.

"I took the disks Bob had made home and thought I would watch the movies anyway. I wanted to see if the 3-D DVDs could play in a regular DVD player. I popped *Dracula* in and it seemed to play all right. The only problem was that Dracula was missing."

"What?" Bob said, sitting up.

Nina laughed. "Okay, now I think *both* of you landed on your heads."

"Dracula was missing," Joe continued. "I thought it was just a glitch at first. I stopped the player and started it again. All the other characters were in the movie, but Dracula was gone."

"What do you mean 'gone'?" Nina said.

"Gone," Joe replied. "Not there."

Nina raised her arms in exasperation. "I don't know what you're saying."

Joe sighed. "Dracula has disappeared from his movie."

"Wow!" Bob exclaimed.

"You guys, stop trying to freak me out," Nina said.

"I checked. At first I thought it was just a glitch in the DVD or my DVD player." Joe said. "I used a virus program to check the disk for viruses and distortions. The disk is fine. Nothing unusual. I put the disk back in the player. The credits came on, the characters came on, but Count Dracula was missing. The other characters were moving about just like they're supposed to do, but Dracula wasn't there." Joe swallowed. "I ran a binary-imagery check. It took me three weeks. That's why I didn't say anything."

Nina's face was red. She crossed her arms. "I like you, Joe, but I'm getting a little upset because I don't know what you're trying to say."

"The binary code for the Dracula character was missing, right?" Bob chimed in.

"Right," Joe said. "Dracula is no longer in his movie."

Bob's eyes flashed with excitement. "You know, lightning did hit the house. That's what blew up the projector. Remember how the Dracula character looked at us just before the projector blew up? I could swear he was looking right at me, trying to tell me something. Then he reached for Nina, and disappeared. And remember the black, white, and gray stream that seemed to pour from the projector?"

"Yeah," Joe said. "That's what happened."

Nina threw her arms up. "Let me see if I understand this train of thought: We were watching *Dracula*, lightning hit the house, the projector blew up, and now the Dracula character is no longer in the movie."

"Yeah," Joe said again.

"So, where is he?" Nina said.

Bob and Joe looked knowingly at each other and then at Nina.

Surprise and realization covered Nina's face. "Oh, no. I refuse to believe this."

"I, uh, think it's true," Joe said.

"Think about it," Bob began. "When did the attack on Todd Gentry and his father happen? A few hours after the storm. The same storm that destroyed the projector. And Todd said he saw a giant wolf, one that stood on his two hind legs like a man. Dracula can transform himself into a giant wolf."

"And the murders along I-95 began a few nights later," Joe added.

"Wait a minute," Nina protested. "I thought you guys believed that Slice was involved in some sort of vampire cult and was behind the murders."

"We still do," Bob said, looking at Joe. Joe nodded.

"I know it sounds crazy," Joe said to Nina. "There's something else I didn't tell you. The projector we took was the bad prototype. It wasn't supposed to work. Apparently, the program changes I made in the projector fixed the problem *too* well."

"Wow!" Bob said. "This is just like in *Frankenstein* when Fritz steals the bad brain."

Nina stared at Bob, then at Joe. "Look, guys, those are just movies," she said. "How can images on film suddenly come to life?"

Neither Bob nor Joe answered. They all sat in silence.

A loud chirping filled the room. Nina reached into her purse and pulled out her cell phone.

"Hello?" she said into the phone.

Joe leaned closer to Bob, "Are we crazy? Did Dracula really come to life?"

"Hey, I read an article on the Internet that said

that holographic imagery was the next evolutionary step in computer technology. Maybe we've already created it."

"Slow down, Angela," Nina said into the phone.

"Part of me wants to laugh and part of me is scared," Joe admitted.

"Me, too. Those ticks were real, Joe. I wasn't dreaming. I was being attacked by giant, blood-sucking ticks."

"What?" Nina said loudly.

"But Dracula never appeared as a tick," Joe said.

"Hey, this is the twenty-first century," Bob fired back. "I guess he can appear any which way he wants."

"Not you too! Okay, we'll be right over." Nina punched the OFF button on her cell phone. She put the phone back into her purse and pulled out her keys. "Angela says that Devin just attacked her. Devin was too weak, so Angela overpowered her. Now Devin's screaming that the Prince of Darkness, Count Dracula himself, has returned and wants to make her his bride!"

CHAPTER TWELVE
FRIDAY EVENING

"Here," Nina said as she handed Angela a glass of water.

Angela looked up, smiled weakly, and took the glass. She quickly drained its entire contents. "Thank you." She looked up at her friend. Nina smiled. She had never seen Angela look so worried and frightened, not even when they heard the news about Todd's attack.

"Anything else you want?" Nina asked.

"My life to be normal again," Angela replied with a sad smile.

"You sure she's tied up okay?" Joe asked as he looked down at Devin, who appeared to be in a deep sleep.

"Wow!" Bob said. He had leaned over Devin and pulled her lips apart, revealing the long canines. "Those are vampire teeth all right."

"I thought you were in an accident," Angela said.

"He insisted on coming," Nina explained.

Bob straightened up. "I feel fine."

"You don't really think your sister is a vampire, do you, Angela?" Nina said.

"I don't know what to think," Angela said, looking at her sister. Nina looked on, worried, as tears welled in her friend's eyes. "A few days ago, she was telling me how happy she was with her life, her job, that she was going to break it off with Slice and really try to make something of herself. She was even going to let her hair go back to its original color."

"What color is her hair?" Bob said.

"It's blond, like mine," Angela replied.

"Did she say anything before she passed out?" Joe asked.

"Just that Dracula had returned to make her his bride."

"Did she say anything about Slice?" Bob said.

"She mumbled something about Slice and vampires, but I really couldn't understand her. Before she tried to attack me, she said Slice had been waiting for her when Abel dropped her off. She said he kissed her."

Nina knelt in front of her friend. "We've been best friends since junior high. I've always believed you when you told me things. But I'm having a hard time believing this, Angela. I like monsters and all, but they're only in the movies. Devin's probably just got a fever or something and is delirious."

Angela stared hard at Nina, her face blank.

"You think I'm making this up? You think my sister has a fever? You think Devin grew fangs and is playing a joke on all of us?"

Nina was about to say no when Angela sprang up from the chair and stomped over to the closed curtains covering the large picture window. "You think this is a joke?" She grabbed the cord and pulled. The drapes flew open.

Light from the bright setting sun poured into the room, momentarily blinding Nina, Joe, and Bob.

A soft moan filled the room. They all glanced at Devin. Her eyes were still closed and she appeared to be asleep, but her body was moving, pulling against the cords that Angela had bound her with.

Nina gasped. Devin's skin was white and pulled tight. Dark blue veins in her arms and neck and face pulsed as blood pumped through them. Devin's face contorted with pain.

"Look!" Bob said, pointing at Devin's arms.

The skin rippled in the light of the sun, like small waves in a stream. Wave after wave flowed up her arms and neck and across her face. She twisted in pain.

Suddenly, Devin's eyes snapped open. They were a luminous yellow. Devin stared at Bob and hissed, her fangs dripping with saliva. Bob took a step toward her to get a closer look. She snapped at him.

"Whoa!" Bob said, jumping back.

The room went black as Angela quickly closed the curtains.

"Yeah," Angela said, turning on a floor lamp. Devin had fainted and sat silent and still in the chair. "This is all make-believe, just like in the movies." She buried her face in her hands and sobbed.

Nina ran to her friend and put her arms around her.

"I'd say we have a serious case of vampirism," Bob said. "Do you have any garlic, Angela?"

"What?" Angela said, lifting her head, her eyes red, tears streaming down her face.

"Garlic," Bob replied. "Vampires are allergic to garlic."

"Knock it off, Bob," Nina said.

"I'm serious," Bob said. "The only way to keep Devin under control is to keep garlic around her."

"Look at this," Joe said loudly.

Bob turned to see his friend remove Devin's black choker with the dragon clasp. Two reddish-blue, pencil-sized holes on the left side of Devin's neck were revealed.

"This confirms it," Joe announced.

"No!" Angela cried.

Nina led her friend to the couch and sat her down. Angela fell onto the couch, crying. Nina crossed to Bob and Joe, and the three huddled together, talking quietly.

"Okay, guys," Nina said. "I'm not sure what to believe. I don't know if I believe in your Count-Dracula-comes-to-life theory, but something is happening here, and we've got to help Angela and Devin."

"I say we find Slice and drive a stake through his heart," Bob said.

Nina frowned. "We don't even know if he is the vampire. Besides, how can he be Dracula? We've known Slice for a long time."

"Maybe Dracula has possessed Slice," Bob suggested. "Slice would be the perfect candidate: He's not too bright, doesn't like daylight, and he already had that devil-may-care vampire look."

"He *does* look like a vampire," Joe admitted.

"No, wait," Bob said, thinking. "I've seen him eat garlic."

"What?" Nina said.

"He's been in Beach Burger a few times and always orders his hamburgers with garlic. Vampires can't stand garlic," Bob explained.

Nina rolled her eyes.

"But have you seen him eat a garlic hamburger since the night of the storm?" Joe asked.

"Hey, you're right!" Bob said. "He's been gone with his band for the past month. That's when the projector blew up and Todd was attacked and the murders began. Last night was the first time he's been in the Beach Burger for over a month. And did you see how he picked me up off the floor? I say we find Slice and rub garlic all over him and watch him scream."

"I say we call Detective Turner and let him handle it," Joe said.

"And tell him what?" Nina said. "That Slice is possessed by Dracula, who happened to escape from a 3-D movie projector during a lightning storm and is now terrorizing San Tomas Inlet instead of London?"

Bob and Joe looked at each other, saying nothing.

Bob shrugged. "Okay. Back to Plan A: We find Slice and drive a stake through his heart."

"No one's going to drive a stake through anybody's heart!" Nina insisted.

"I don't think that's such a bad idea." The group was startled to find Angela standing behind them.

"You shouldn't be up," Nina said.

"I'm fine," Angela said, brushing tears from her face. Her color had returned and she looked determined. "I've been listening. I know it's crazy, but I believe Bob is right: Slice is a vampire and he has to be destroyed."

"We're not going to destroy anyone," Nina said.

Bob turned to Angela. "Do you have any garlic?"

"We've got some cloves of garlic and a hammer and some tent stakes. Will they do?" Angela asked.

"Guys, we are not going to drive a stake through Slice's heart!" Nina said.

A scream filled the room. They turned just in time to see Devin sitting up in the chair. Her pupils were fiery red floating in black circles. Her skin was ashen gray. Her mouth was open wide, revealing fangs and an entire mouth of sharp, pointy teeth.

Devin struggled against the cords that bound her hands and arms to the chair. She screamed and hissed at the four teens as she pulled against the ropes. A sudden wind whipped through the room. Papers flew about. Books flew open, the pages fluttering. The chair began to rock back and forth as she struggled against the cords. The legs of the chair pounded on the hardwood floor like a jackhammer on concrete.

"I'm getting the garlic!" Bob shouted. He disappeared into the kitchen.

"No!" Angela screamed, reaching out to her sister.

"Angela!" Nina grabbed her friend and held her back.

Joe stepped forward and seized the arms of the chair to keep it from rocking. He was afraid it would fall over and Devin would hurt herself.

Devin hissed and spit at Joe. Then one arm broke free of the cords. She grabbed Joe by the throat and tossed him across the room. Joe landed on the couch with such force that it tumbled over backward and he disappeared behind it.

Devin tore the remaining cords holding her

down and floated from the chair. She spread her arms toward Nina and Angela. The two girls backed up to the room's entrance.

"No!" Angela screamed over and over.

"We've got to run!" Nina shouted over Angela's cries. She was holding on to her struggling friend, trying to keep her away from her sister.

"I've got the garlic!" Bob shouted as he ran back into the room, holding up a small head of garlic in his right hand. "WHOA!" He tried to stop himself, but his shoes slipped on the waxed wooden floorboards and he slid right into Devin, wrapping his arms around her to keep himself from falling.

The pair flew across the room and hit a far wall covered with family photos. They fell to the ground, with Devin landing on top of Bob. Photos and glass hit the ground all around them.

Devin grabbed Bob's wrists and pinned his arms to the floor. He looked up into her eyes. The face of death stared back at him.

"I understand you like to ride motorcycles," Devin said, but the voice wasn't hers. Nor was it one voice. It sounded as though several voices were speaking through her. "Did you like my friends that I sent to you?"

Bob struggled, trying to get his arms free. "YOU sent the ticks?"

"Yes," the multitude of voices replied. "They enjoyed riding with you." Devin's face grew stern. "You didn't have to kill my friends!"

Bob tried bucking Devin off him. Devin sat down hard on his chest, knocking the air out of him. Bob groaned and gasped for breath.

"You didn't have to kill my friends!" Devin repeated. "Now you will join them." She opened her mouth and slowly leaned down, moving closer to Bob's throat and the vein that pulsed through his skin.

Bob struggled, but Devin was too strong for him. He grimaced as her mouth came closer to his face. He had never smelled vampire breath before, but the stench that came from Devin's mouth was similar to the smell of rotting fish. He couldn't believe that a girl was beating him up. He'd never live it down at school. If he lived through this at all.

Then he remembered the small clove of garlic in his hand. "Hungry for a little garlic?" he groaned, tossing the clove toward Devin's face. But Devin held his wrist down so tightly that the garlic sailed into the air a few inches, then plopped down near his armpit.

"Air ball," Devin said with a laugh. "Now, let's finish the game with a slam dunk."

Bob struggled as Devin's mouth inched closer to his throat. Her long, jet-black hair fell over his face, blinding him. He could feel her hot breath on his throat and the icy-cold saliva that dripped from her razor-sharp fangs.

CHAPTER THIRTEEN

Bob heard a scream. He was pretty sure it was coming from his own throat. Then, through the black strands of Devin's hair, he saw a blurred hand pressing something against her forehead. The screaming continued, but Bob realized it wasn't him after all. He heard a hissing, and smelled something burning. A pungent smell. He had smelled the same odor a couple of years earlier when he had gone camping and tripped over the campfire, landing on a log that was red-hot.

It was the smell of burning flesh that filled the air.

The pressure on Bob's chest and wrists gave way. The screaming stopped and Devin toppled next to him in a heap.

Bob scrambled to his feet, his breathing heavy. Joe stood over him, holding a small cross attached to a silver chain. Bob looked down at Devin. There was a burn mark in the shape of a cross in the middle of her forehead.

"Where? What?" Bob gasped between breaths.

"My grandma gave it to me last Christmas. I forgot I had it on until Devin threw me into the couch. You better do something about that," Joe said, pointing to Bob's throat.

Bob's hand went to his neck. He felt something sticky. He looked at his fingers and gasped when he saw a small spot of blood. He picked up the small clove of garlic and put it against the wound.

"I think she just scratched the surface," Joe said. "I wouldn't worry."

"Of course you wouldn't worry," Bob said. "You're not going to turn into a vampire and start drinking the blood of your friends. I can't become a vampire! I don't even like staying up late at night and I can't stand sleeping in a coffin. You know I have claustrophobia!"

"Is — she — dead?" Angela asked, sobbing.

"No," Joe answered. "But we've got to make sure she doesn't attack anyone else."

"What do we do?" Bob said.

"We've got to get her up to her bedroom and surround her with garlic," Nina said decisively.

Angela, Bob, and Joe stared at Nina incredulously. Nina sighed and shrugged.

"All right," she finally said. "I'm still not sure I believe you guys, but I believe she believes she's a vampire, and I believe Slice is involved, too."

"I'm a believer," Bob said, pressing the garlic tightly against his neck.

"And if — and that's a big IF — Slice is possessed by Dracula, then we already know how to defeat him: garlic, holy water, cross, Communion wafers, all the things that evil hates — just like in the movie," Nina continued.

"And the hammer and the stakes and —" Joe began.

"No!" Nina interrupted. She looked at Joe. "Think you can carry Devin upstairs?"

"Sure," Joe said.

"But do you want to?" Bob said, his eyes wide.

"You going to do it?" Nina asked Bob.

"Hey, I think I've done my fair share of vampire fighting for the day," Bob replied.

Joe put his cross around his neck, leaving it out over his shirt. "I'll be all right." He knelt down, scooped Devin into his arms, and rose without effort. "You'll have to show me the way," he said to Angela.

"Upstairs," Angela replied. She led them into the hallway and up the stairs.

"Jeez, this room would qualify for a spread in *Better Tombs and Graveyards*," Bob said, following his friends into Devin's room.

The room was painted black from floor to ceiling. A black light cast a bluish hue, and fluorescent posters of dragons, warlocks, warriors, ogres, elves, gremlins, and flying horses stood out like ghosts suspended in the air. Angela flipped on the bedroom's overhead light, washing away the posters' magic.

The teens blinked as their eyes adjusted to the light. Joe lay Devin on the bed.

"We've got to make sure she's safe until we find Slice," Nina said. "Do you have any more garlic?" she asked Angela.

"I don't know. I don't cook," Angela said. "I'll go look." She turned and left the room.

"Keep her company, Bob," Nina said. "We'll stay here with Devin."

Bob was staring at a poster of a beautiful female warrior swinging a sword at a particularly nasty-looking werewolf. "Huh?" he said, without taking his eyes off the poster.

"Put your eyes back in your head, and go downstairs to help Angela look for more garlic."

"Yeah. Sure. Okay." Bob backed out of the room without turning away from the poster of the woman warrior. Suddenly Nina stood in front of him. Bob shook his head, clearing his mind. "Yeah. Downstairs." He leaned to one side to get a last glance at the woman warrior.

"Now!" Nina said. Bob disappeared down the stairs.

Joe removed his silver cross and chain and placed them near Devin.

"Will that be enough?" Nina said, perching on the edge of the bed.

"This and the garlic ought to do it."

"I might buy the vampire cult theory, Joe, but I'm still not so sure about Dracula leaping out of a seventy-year-old movie, coming to life, and possessing Slice."

Joe continued gazing at Devin. Except for the snow-white skin and dark circles around her eyes, she looked like any normal person sleeping. "Well, the purpose of the 3-D projector is to turn two-dimensional images into realistic, lifelike images. I know it sounds impossible. But, imagine telling your great-grandfather a hundred years ago that one day his great-granddaughter would sit down at a machine and be able to talk with anyone in the world at the speed of light."

"I know," Nina said with a sigh. "Some of the world's greatest advancements have come through simple mistakes. But this isn't like discovering the theory of gravity or accidentally inventing the glue on yellow sticky pads. You and Bob are claiming that a living, breathing movie monster has entered the real world."

"I know it sounds crazy, but —"

"Let's say for the sake of argument that I accept your hypothesis. Let's say Dracula really is lurking around out there and Devin is one of his victims. Why didn't he kill her like he did the others on I-95? And the original *Dracula* was made in 1931. How could he know how to act and behave and get along in the twenty-first century?"

"Maybe," Bob piped up from the doorway, "while we're watching the characters in the movies, the characters are watching us. Maybe reality isn't what it's cracked up to be."

"Maybe *you're* cracked," Nina said, her eyebrows raised.

"What are you talking about?" Angela said, coming back into the room.

"We think we accidentally released the real Dracula into the twenty-first century," Nina replied.

"What?"

"Well," Bob said as he moved to the bed, his hands full of garlic cloves, "not the real Dracula. There never was a real Dracula. He's just a myth. But the Dracula character from the 1931 version of *Dracula*." He began laying the cloves in an outline around Devin's body.

Angela stood silently for several moments. She looked from Joe to Nina to Bob and then finally to her sister. At last she said, "I don't know what's going on. All I know is that my sister is a vampire, and I want her back to her normal red-lipstick, black-fingernails, jet-black-hair Goth self. If that means that Dracula is alive and we have to kill him, then so be it."

Nina could see the sincerity in her friend's eyes. She breathed deeply. How many nights had she sat at dinner with her father and heard him talk about the lightning-fast advances in computer technology and programming? If anybody knew about the advancements in computer technology, it would be her father. He was the founder and chief software developer of New World Systems, a leader in mainframe microsystems and DNA chip technology. Some of the advancements that were just around the corner included teletransportation that could move people and objects great distances in the blink of an eye; holographic images that looked as real as reality itself; and nano-computers that could enter the body and fight against diseases like cancer. None of these was the stuff of science fiction any longer. Scientists were working daily to bring such fantastic ideas to reality. Some of the greatest advancements in human science and technology occurred through simple accidents, her father had said many times over. Who knows? Maybe the next great advancement will come from some kid playing on his computer with a simple software program.

And, Nina thought, *maybe that is just what has happened.*

Nina jumped up from the bed, startling the other three. "We've got to find Slice. If he's been turned into Dracula, we've got to stop him before he kills anybody else. I think the only reason he didn't kill Devin is because the real Slice has feelings for her and Dracula-Slice couldn't overcome those feelings."

"You think that's possible?" Bob said.

"What?" Nina said.

"That a creep like Slice would have any idea what true love is?"

"Angela."

They all turned to discover that Devin's eyes were open and she was moving her lips.

"Angela." Her voice was weak and hoarse. "Angel Girl."

Angela sat on the edge of the bed, holding her sister's hand.

"Wow," Bob said softly. Devin's skin had regained some color and the veins could no longer be seen through her skin. Her irises had reverted back to their usual blue. Beads of sweat popped up on Devin's forehead. "The undead don't sweat, I'm sure of it," Bob said.

"Yes, Devin," Angela said softly.

"I'm sorry." Devin coughed. "He promised me —" and she coughed again. "For you. Protect you. I'm sorry." Then her eyes closed and her head fell to the side. She breathed deeply, but her face looked troubled, like she was having a bad dream.

Angela leaned forward and kissed her sister on the forehead. "It's okay, big sister. We'll bring you back." She stroked Devin's hair, which was saturated with sweat. "We'll bring you back." She stood and faced Nina, Bob, and Joe. "What do we do to save my sister? Tell me."

"The first thing we do is find Slice," Nina said.

"Once we find him, we have to figure out a way to rid the vampire from him," Joe added.

"I say put a stake through his heart," Bob said, adjusting the hat on his head.

Nina looked at Bob. "We just might have to put a stake through his heart. Any idea how we're going to do that?"

"I'll do it," Angela said, her voice low and determined. "Slice is trying to turn my sister into one of the undead, and he tried to kill Todd." She took a deep breath. "I'll hold the stake and drive it through his black heart with the hammer!"

CHAPTER FOURTEEN
FRIDAY NIGHT, 9:30 p.m.

Impossible, Nina thought as she drove through the dark streets of San Tomas Inlet. *I can't believe I'm doing this. Vampires, movie monsters coming to life, people floating in the air. The next thing you know, I'll start believing in Santa Claus again.*

Did I ever really stop believing in Santa Claus?

Maybe the reality of Santa Claus, but certainly not the idea of Santa Claus. Not the idea that we ought to try to bring happiness and joy to others. Not the idea that all humankind ought to work in harmony and peace to try to provide a better life for us and for the children of the future. That we ought to —

Nina interrupted her thoughts with a laugh. *Santa Claus was no more real than — Count Dracula.*

Yes, Virginia, there really is a Count Dracula. And he lives in the black hearts of evil men everywhere.

A gust of cool air flew in through her open window. The night air was chilly. Nina shivered. She had the top closed on her convertible. She wished she had put it down at the grocery store. The passenger seat was filled with the strong scent of raw garlic. Strings of garlic. All she could find. Some to put around Devin to protect her in case Slice appeared, and some to take with them in case they found Slice and needed to subdue him.

She thought about hitting the button that would lower the convertible top, but decided against it. She was only a few miles from Angela's house. Besides, the wind was growing colder by the minute.

She felt herself jerked forward. "Hey!" Nina glanced in her rearview mirror. She had been so deep in thought that she hadn't seen headlights approaching her. They were right on her bumper. Then the lights lurched forward and the car hit her again. "HEY!"

Nina sped up a little. Perhaps the driver just wanted to pass her. The car behind her sped up also, staying right on her bumper. Nina stuck her arm out the driver's window and motioned for the car to pass her. In response, the car lunged forward and struck her again.

All right. You want to play it that way, hot shot? Nina pushed down on the gas pedal again. The Camaro jumped forward and moved away from the following car, the headlights growing smaller in her rearview mirror. For a moment, it looked as though she would outpace the car. But suddenly the car's headlights grew closer and the vehicle was on Nina's bumper once more. She heard a roar and saw the car jump. This time the bump was more violent than before.

"I've had just about enough of this," Nina said between gritted teeth. She stomped the accelerator down to the floor. The Camaro roared to life. It instantly kicked into high gear and sped away from the offending car.

Nina spotted an empty parking lot. Maybe she could lose the other car by pulling off the road. She killed her lights and steered the car into the lot, then turned the wheel sharply. The wheels squealed against the asphalt pavement as the car spun around. Nina hit the brakes, and the Camaro came to a sudden halt, the engine purring like a lion watching distant prey.

A second later, the black car roared passed the parking lot. Then it squealed to a stop, backed up, and turned into the parking lot, its bright headlights reflecting off Nina's white Camaro.

"What does this pinhead want?" Nina said aloud nervously, turning her headlights back on.

The black car stopped several yards from Nina's. The engine roared as though answering Nina's question.

"I'm waitin' for ya, buddy," Nina said in reply. If only the other driver would get out of his car — then she could stomp on the accelerator and leave him behind.

The car's door opened and a tall, thin man stepped out. "Hey," Slice yelled as he slammed the door shut. "I just want to talk to you." He walked to the front of his car, standing between both vehicles, his headlights giving him an eerie white outline.

A cold shiver caressed Nina's spine and for a brief moment, she wished she had just kept on driving to Angela's. If all this talk about vampires was true, then Slice was their prime suspect, and Nina didn't feel too comfortable sitting in the middle of a dark, empty parking lot in the middle of the night with little more than her wits and a seat full of garlic to protect her.

"Hey!" Slice repeated.

"What do you want?" Nina yelled from the front seat. She kept her window rolled down, but she wasn't about to get out. She had the advantage of being in her car with the engine running. If Slice so much as sneered at her, she was going to floor the accelerator and head to Angela's.

"I just want to ask you a question," Slice said, approaching the driver's door.

Nina could tell he was trying his best to sound sincere. But it came off like a rattlesnake trying to smile while rattling its tail.

"Ask it," Nina said, hoping she sounded normal.

"Where's Devin?"

"Why do you ask?"

"I've got a message for her."

"What is the message?"

"Tell her — I *misssss* her," he replied, hissing.

"Sure, I'll tell her that. Right after I tell her that you tried to kill me by running me off the road!"

"You tell her I better hear from her, or her doctor friend might have a little accident."

"You mean like the accident you wanted me to have? Are you crazy bumping into me like that? You could have killed me."

Slice smiled. "Not an unpleasant image, if you ask me." He leaned down to the window to leer at her.

Nina recoiled. "Just stay away from me."

"Listen, you little punk —"

Nina laughed. "You're calling me a punk? You're a poor excuse for a Halloween mask."

Slice's eyes glowed with anger. Suddenly, his arm shot out, fast as lightning.

"Gotcha!" he said, grabbing her arm through the window.

Nina tried to pull away, but Slice was strong for someone so skinny. "Get your grimy hands off me and off my car." She threw all her weight against the car door, so it jerked open suddenly.

The door caught Slice in the stomach. But instead of releasing Nina, his grip tightened around her and she spilled out of the car. They both tumbled to the ground, rolling for several yards as each tried to get an advantage over the other.

They finally stopped, with Nina on the bottom. Slice was just too strong for her. A cold hand grabbed her by the throat, squeezing her windpipe. She tried to roll away, but Slice clamped down harder, cutting her air off. She tried to take a deep breath, but could do little more than gasp.

"Want to have a little fun and games, do we?" Slice asked, his hot breath hitting her face.

Nina flailed her arms at Slice's neck and face, but nothing seemed to affect him. He possessed an unnatural strength. The strength of a vampire.

Nina grabbed Slice's left ear. She felt his trademark pentagram earring and yanked.

Slice yelled as the earring tore through his earlobe.

Sensing her advantage, Nina landed a right cross to Slice's left cheek. He tumbled off her.

Nina scrambled to her feet and dashed to her car. She turned slightly to see Slice right behind her. She grabbed the car handle and swung the door with all her might. It slammed into Slice. He moaned, but managed to grab her shoulder and break his fall.

"That was my favorite earring," he said, grunting and spitting. "You'll pay for that."

Nina reached into the car and spun around quickly. "Here's the first installment, you pig!" She smashed a string of garlic into his face and rubbed it in with all her might.

Slice screamed as the garlic burned into his skin. He released her.

Nina swung the door once more, this time slamming it into Slice's knees. A sickening crack filled the air. Slice fell to the ground, whimpering.

Without hesitation, Nina jumped into the Camaro and slammed the door shut. She was glad she hadn't turned off the engine. She pushed the console gearshift into reverse and stomped on the accelerator. The tires squealed as all 250 horses of the engine's power were transferred to the wheels. The smell of burnt rubber filled the air.

Slice had jumped to his feet and was chasing after her, limping as he ran. *No man — living or undead — can outrun a Camaro,* Nina thought as she flew out into the street and turned the car toward Angela's house.

She looked into her rearview mirror and saw an angry Slice shaking his fist, growing smaller and smaller in the dimness of the streetlights.

Nina kept checking her rearview mirror, but no headlights appeared. Slice hadn't followed her. Still, she decided to take the long way to Angela's house just in case Slice figured out her destination. She turned onto Beach Front Road.

Now that she'd gotten away from Slice, Nina realized how lucky she'd been. She was still amazed at Slice's strength. He was nearly six feet tall, but he couldn't weigh more than 150 pounds. If anything, he looked like a walking skeleton.

So, Slice reacted violently to garlic, Nina thought.

That was proof enough for her that he was the vampire they were looking for.

Nina felt something tickling the back of her neck. She reached behind her to scratch it. A piercing pain shot through her hand. She pulled her hand back and looked at it. Small bubbles of blood an inch apart shown in the dull dashboard lights.

She looked in the rearview mirror. Two small yellow eyes stared back at her. Then she saw the leathery wings and the small hairy body of a bat.

A mouselike squeal filled the car. Nina felt a sharp pain on the back of her neck, as though someone were jabbing her with syringe needles.

She screamed and hit at the bat with one hand while trying to keep the car steady with the other. The bat's clawed feet dug into her shoulder and its sharp teeth sunk into her neck.

The more she tried to defend herself, the more the bat struck at her. Finally, Nina managed to pull it from her neck and fling it out the open passenger window.

She grabbed the back of her neck and felt the warm, sticky ooze of her own blood. She had to make it back to Angela's before she passed out.

An ear-piercing, high-pitched scream filled the air. The bat dove in through the open window and sunk its teeth into her throat once more.

Nina screamed, losing control of the car. The Camaro swerved and then flew from the road, hitting the sandy beach with a thud. The rear wheels spun in the soft sand until they finally grabbed hold of solid ground and propelled the car toward the dark ocean.

CHAPTER FIFTEEN
M!DN!GHT

Bob felt his eyelids getting heavier. He had tried everything he could to stay awake. He had splashed cold water on his face. He had turned up the volume on his CD player as loud as his ears could stand. He had walked up and down the hallway in front of Devin's room. He had slapped himself in the face. He had taped his eyelids open. Nothing worked.

The only thing keeping Bob awake was his concern for Nina. She should have been back earlier. He had tried calling her on her cell phone, but kept getting an "Out of Area" notice. *Strange,* Bob thought, *where could Nina be in San Tomas Inlet that she would be out of area? Perhaps I'm just dialing it wrong.*

He tried dialing the cell phone two more times, with the same results.

He thought about waking Joe up. Joe had fallen asleep an hour earlier, curling up at the foot of

Devin's bed. Devin was fast asleep, and Angela was sleeping soundly in her own room.

Angela was planning to visit Todd in the hospital first thing in the morning. She was worried that Slice might attack him again and finish the job this time. Bob convinced her to get a couple hours of sleep first. He promised to wake her up in time to visit Todd. Her eyes reddened by tears and exhaustion, Angela had agreed.

Bob had decided that he would stay awake until Nina returned. She was just supposed to pick up as much garlic as possible and then come right back. Bob wasn't sure if the garlic they had set around Devin would be enough to hold off an attack.

The hallway light streamed into the bedroom through the doorway and rested on the sleeping Devin. Joe's cross draped around her neck, the bright silver chain and cross shining brightly against her dark clothes.

Finally, Bob threw himself into a corner chair, pulled his yacht captain's hat down over his eyes, and let his heavy eyelids close. He decided to shut his eyes but to stay awake, to think, to try to figure out how they could get Count Dracula back into his movie.

The whole scenario seemed crazy to him, like some wild dream or fantastic movie. His mind raced through the events of the past month: the job at Universal Studios, the projector, the storm, the attack on Todd Gentry and his father, the murders, Slice's interest in vampirism, and the attack of the giant ticks.

Bob felt a tickle on his arm.

He started and jumped up from the chair, brushing at his arms. He darted into the hallway, holding his arms in front of him. Nothing. No ticks. He tilted his hat back, shook his head, and rubbed his eyes. He decided to check out what the Chavarrias had in the refrigerator. Maybe food would keep him awake.

Bob trotted down the stairs to the kitchen and opened the refrigerator. The bright light of the refrigerator momentarily blinded him. He felt a pang in his stomach. He had not realized how hungry he was until he spotted the food. Bob grabbed a package of ham, cheese slices, and a loaf of wheat bread. He left the door open to provide enough light to see by. He hummed a tune as he fumbled through the pantry and finally pulled out a jar of peanut butter.

Despite the seriousness of his mood, he couldn't help a silent laugh to himself as he recalled Nina's reaction the first time he'd made his famous peanut butter and ham with cheese sandwich in front of her. He had explained that he had invented the sandwich when he'd run out of mayonnaise and used peanut butter instead. Since then, Bob used peanut butter on many of his sandwiches: ham, salami, bologna, turkey.

He made a triple-decker peanut butter, ham, and cheese on whole wheat, and took a big bite. He smacked his lips as he chewed. Then he realized that no sandwich would be complete without a beverage. He glanced around the refrigerator: orange juice, diet soft drinks, tea, and some blue stuff. No bottled water.

He put the half-eaten sandwich down on the counter and searched the cabinets until he found the glasses. Then he went over to the sink. He turned on the tap. When the cup was half full, he raised it to his mouth and drank deeply.

He stared at the bottom of the cup as he drank, watching the water roll back and forth as he gulped. Through the thick glass bottom he spotted two yellow lights. He lowered the cup. The yellow lights remained.

Then the lights flickered. Rather, they blinked. Bob suddenly realized that they weren't lights at all. They were eyes — bright yellow, almond-shaped eyes. They blinked again.

With horror, Bob realized he could see the silhouette of a man standing outside, staring back at him. Bob swallowed. Then the man flew straight up into the air. Bob leaned over to watch the dark figure glide up to the second floor of the Chavarria home. To Devin's room!

Bob ran out of the kitchen and up the stairs. He dashed into Devin's room. He was about to shout to Joe, to wake him up, to warn him about the intruder. But the room was empty except for Devin and Joe, who were both sound asleep. The only sound was Joe's snoring.

Bob shook his head. He felt the hair on his arms and the back of his neck stand on end. He scanned the room quickly, imagining movement everywhere. A slight chill brought goosebumps to his skin, and he shivered.

A moan came from the hallway. Bob walked quickly to the doorway, turning and looking up and down the hall. No one. The moan came again. He looked at the door to Angela's bedroom.

Bob stepped across the hallway and placed his hand on the doorknob. It was ice cold. He quickly released it. Bob wrapped his hand in the bottom of his T-shirt and turned the knob.

An icy wind shot from the room as Bob eased the door open. He pushed hard against it. Light from the hall spilled into the room. The window across from the door was ajar, the curtain fluttering slightly in the wind. Bob stepped in. He could see his breath. He glanced over at the bed. Angela was still dressed, curled up into a ball, her back to Bob and the door. She moaned. *Perhaps,* Bob thought, *she is just having a bad dream.*

He walked over to the window and pulled it down. Bob looked out at the ocean, at the full moon that hung just above the horizon. He had to get some sleep.

He turned and found himself staring into two

large yellow eyes. A dark figure stood between him and the open door.

Bob started to yell, but was cut short by a large hand that grabbed him by the throat. He felt his feet lift from the floor. A hot stench hit his face as he was raised to eye level with the intruder.

Bob dangled in the air, his legs kicking, his throat beginning to burn. He grabbed the man's wrist with one hand while he dug in his pocket with the other. He pulled out a clove of garlic and shoved it in the attacker's face.

The attacker yelled and released him. Bob fell to the floor. He tried to yell, but no sounds came out. His throat was on fire. He crawled to the door. It slammed shut just before he reached it. He jumped to his feet and turned.

The room was dim, the only light coming from the full moon outside the window. He couldn't see the intruder, but he could feel his presence.

"All right, Slice," Bob said. "The game's over. We know what you are." Bob held the garlic out in front of him.

A hiss filled the room. Then the room seemed to get colder.

"Be a nice little vampire," Bob said. "We've got garlic and a cross."

From the corner of his eye, Bob saw a dark shadow move swiftly toward him. Something hard slapped his wrist. The garlic flew from his hand and into the darkness. A dark shadow stepped in front of him. It reached out and grabbed Bob by the front of his shirt. Bob felt himself being thrown backward, striking the door with such force that he bounced back toward the dark figure. He slammed into the intruder and the two fell to the floor. Somehow, Bob landed on top of the vampire. He quickly straddled the intruder's chest and grabbed him by the throat.

"Had enough?" Bob asked as he squeezed.

At least he tried to squeeze. It felt as though he'd grabbed a thick iron post rather than a flesh-and-blood neck. The yellow eyes glared back at him. A low, guttural sound echoed through the room. Bob felt the intruder's throat bulge and contract and bulge again. A hiss issued from the attacker's mouth, and Bob grimaced at the foul breath.

Bob kept one hand on the vampire's throat and raised his right fist over his head. If he couldn't strangle the Lord of the Undead, he was going to have to punch his lights out. He swung down as hard as he could.

"OW!" Bob screamed as his fist slammed into the hardwood floor.

The vampire had faded into a red mist that floated above the floor. Bob sat in the middle of the mist, holding his throbbing hand. The mist moved slowly around Bob, encircling him. Bob jumped to his feet when he realized what was happening.

The mist formed a tall column in front of him. The top of the column struck out like a whip and hit Bob in the forehead. Bob yelled from the pain. The mist enveloped him like a shroud, the icy air biting his bare arms and face.

Bob swung out at the mist, his fists flailing wildly through the air. Then an invisible force slapped his arms down to his sides.

The mist began to spin, slowly at first and then faster and faster. Bob tried to escape it, but the harder he tried to move, the more it contracted, like a python suffocating its prey. Bob felt himself start to spin, the soles of his tennis shoes squeaking on the wooden floor.

Bob moaned as he spun faster and faster. He began to feel light-headed. Maybe the peanut butter and ham with cheese on whole wheat hadn't been such a good idea after all.

A blinding light abruptly filled the room. Bob squeezed his eyes shut against the glare. All of a sudden, the force constricting him was gone. Bob pirouetted and turned around, falling to the floor flat on his back.

He kept his eyes closed. He knew he was lying down, but he felt as though he were still spinning. Through his dizziness, he heard grunts and groans and growls and the sounds of furniture smashing.

He slowly sat up and opened his eyes.

The room still twirled around him. But through his dizziness, Bob could see Joe wrestling with a giant wolf. The big freshman had the wolf in a headlock. It was bucking its head, trying to throw Joe.

Bob scrambled to his feet and ran to help his friend. The room tilted around him. He staggered forward. Joe and the wolf were a blur.

Bob felt a lump in his stomach that began to push its way upward. Stinging acid ate at the back of his throat. He stumbled forward, close enough to grab the wolf. He reached out.

The wolf lurched forward in an effort to wrest itself from Joe's stranglehold. Its head butted into Bob's stomach, and before he could stop himself, Bob threw up all over the wolf and Joe.

Bob fell backward, hitting the floor with a thud. He smacked his lips and shook his head. His vision cleared.

Joe and the wolf were momentarily still. Joe's face was twisted in disgust and disbelief as he brushed the front of his shirt.

The wolf shook its head and gagged.

"Hey!"

Bob turned and saw Devin standing in the doorway. Her pale skin shone in the bright light. She held the silver cross that hung about her neck in front of her. She moved slowly but surely toward the giant wolf.

The wolf growled and snapped as Devin moved closer.

"You can't have her," Devin said slowly. She stumbled, but held the cross straight ahead of her.

The wolf backed up against the wall, just under the window. Its black lips were pulled back over its sharp yellow teeth. Its hate-filled eyes bored into Devin. Bob could see that Devin was using every ounce of strength she had to keep the cross held in front of her.

The wolf suddenly leaped. Bob tried to get to his feet to protect Devin, but he was still too weak. He fell back to the floor. He could see that the wolf hadn't attacked Devin. It had leaped straight up into the air and transformed into a giant bat.

The bat's wings spanned at least seven feet. It flapped its wings furiously, hovering just inches above the floor. The force of wind was so strong it created a near-hurricane gale. Devin screamed as she struggled to press forward, her black hair flowing straight behind her. Pictures and posters on the wall flew into the air.

Joe ducked and covered his face to protect himself. A thick American literature book flew from Angela's backpack and struck him on the side of his head. He fell to the floor and didn't move.

The whirlwind created a tornado of spinning objects around the room — clothes, magazines, photos, stuffed animals, paper. It pressed Bob back to the floor. The icy draft cut him to the bone.

"You can't have her!" Devin cried again. But she was thrown out the door with one swift, strong thrust of the bat's wings.

"No!" she screamed. The door slammed shut behind her.

The bat ceased its flapping and touched lightly to

the floor. Bob, sickness still floating in his stomach and throat, watched as the six-foot human-bat walked gently to the still-sleeping Angela.

The wings of the bat folded and pressed against the monster's back. Bob tried to sit up. The bat turned at the movement, its hellish yellow eyes glowering at the teen. It hissed, showing long, sharp teeth that dripped with saliva. Its face and body were part human, part bat. Bob felt a new sickness rising within him as he stared in terror at the vampire, whose skin was rotting and peeling away, hanging like torn cloth from exposed bones.

Bob slumped back against the floor, his head turned slightly toward the vampire.

The bat turned back to Angela, whose peaceful sleep and calm breathing belied the horror that threatened her. The vampire reached out with decaying, bony fingers. He gently stroked the sleeping girl's blond hair.

"No," Bob said weakly, but he couldn't move. Pain, exhaustion, and terror had sapped all his strength.

The vampire ignored Bob. It closed its eyes, shuddered, and disappeared, transforming into the red mist that had attacked Bob. The mist slowly floated and hovered over Angela. Then it lowered, covering her in a transparent shroud.

Bob was unsure of what happened next. His vision began to blur, but it looked as though Angela had disappeared into the mist. He watched as the mist floated across the room over the unconscious Joe, over his own helpless body, and into the dark night.

Bob moaned. He closed his eyes and was instantly swimming in black sleep.

CHAPTER SIXTEEN
THE NEXT MORNING

The Chavarria home was dark and quiet as Nina entered through the front door. *Too quiet*, she thought. Her muscles tensed. But just tensing up made every muscle in her body ache. She muttered a silent *ow* and started slowly up the stairs.

Nina knew she was bruised. She hadn't had time to look at herself in the mirror, but she could feel the soreness all over.

Light from upstairs mixed with the rising sun cast an orange-gray shadow down the stairs. The light was coming from Angela's room. Nina peered in. Joe was lying on his stomach next to Angela's bed, his arm crooked in front of him and his head resting on it. He breathed deeply, but not too loudly. Captain Bob was lying face up a few feet from Joe, spread-eagled on the floor. He was snoring loudly.

Angela's bed was empty. In fact, it looked as though no one had slept in it at all.

Nina walked over to Bob and tapped his foot with her toe. "Bob. Wake up."

Bob didn't move.

She tapped the bottom of his foot again. "Hey Bob, wake up."

Bob snorted and twitched his nose.

Nina knelt down next to him. She grabbed his shoulders and gently shook him, picking his head up from the floor. "Bob."

Bob snorted again, but his eyes remained closed.

Nina shook him harder. "Bob!" she said more firmly.

Bob's eyes fluttered, but they did not open.

"*Oh, Mona,*" Bob said, and then snorted. He threw his arms up around Nina and began drawing her closer to him. "Yes, I'll kiss you."

"*What!*" Nina struggled free from Bob's sleepy grasp.

Bob threw his arms around her again. "No. Don't go, Mona. I'll love you forever!" He lifted his head, his eyes still closed, and his lips pushed out like a fish sucking in water.

"*Yuck,*" Nina said, shaking her head. She instinctively let go of Bob and he fell back, his head hitting the varnished floor with a thud.

Bob groaned. Then a smile appeared on his face. He turned over to his side, curled into a fetal position, and started snoring again.

"Forget it," Joe's voice said from behind Nina.

Nina spun around. "Oh, good. At least you're awake."

Joe was leaning against Angela's bed. He rubbed the back of his head and then stretched. "Bob's in dream land. The only thing that could wake him up now is the last school bell of the day."

Nina stood and offered Joe a hand. "You guys turned out to be some watchmen. I can't leave you alone for even a few hours."

"It's a good thing we *were* here," Joe said. "I think Slice tried to get to Devin last night."

"Yeah?" Nina said. "I had a run-in with Slice myself. Where's Angela?"

Joe turned and looked at the bed. "I don't know where she is now. Last night she said something about visiting Todd first thing in the morning. Maybe she got up early and went to the hospital. All I know is that she was here when the giant bat knocked me out. She slept through it all."

"A bat, huh? I was attacked by a bat last night after I ran into Slice."

"Slice or the bat give you that bruise on your forehead?"

"Yes."

"Yes to which one?"

"To both. Slice *as* the bat gave me this bruise." Nina started toward the door. "Let's get some food. I need some juice before I tell you about my run-in with Slice the *vampire*."

Joe raised his eyebrows and followed her from the room.

". . . So then when the bat flew into my car, I turned onto the beach. My car hit a soft spot and just stopped. My head hit the steering wheel and the bat slammed into the windshield. I guess I was stunned, but I recovered quickly and reached for the garlic. The rest is history. The bat . . ." Nina finished.

Joe bit into a slice of jam-covered toast. "You're lucky it didn't attack you again." He looked at both sides of her throat. "No bite marks."

Nina swallowed the last of the orange juice from her glass. "I think the garlic had something to do with it, too."

Joe smiled.

Nina smiled sheepishly back at him. "All right. I'm not saying I totally believe you guys, but that wasn't just any ordinary bat. This thing was *big*."

"I wonder how Slice could have been in two places at once?" Joe asked, his voice far away. "He was here fighting us *and* there attacking."

"Maybe he's got a legion of trained giant bats," Nina replied.

Joe looked at Nina. He pulled at the T-shirt he'd borrowed from Angela's dad's bureau. "That boy owes me a new Hawaiian shirt. How's your car?"

"The car's fine. I thought that the bat was going to eat through my neck. Then I remembered the garlic in the passenger seat. I just grabbed a handful and started rubbing them all over. The bat squealed and flew out of the car."

"Did you see what happened to it?"

Nina shook her head. "I just stomped on the gas pedal and got out of there."

"You need to get those bites looked it. That bat could have rabies," Joe said.

"Oh, great. Not only am I candidate for Queen of the Dead, but I could have rabies as well. That'll look great on my senior transcript."

"I'm guessing that Slice came here to get Devin and that somehow Captain Bob was able to fight him off," Joe said.

"Yeah," Nina said, her face puzzled. "Who would have thought Bob had it in him?"

"What have I got in me?" Bob asked as he entered the kitchen. He sat at the breakfast table, stretched, yawned, and rubbed his eyes. "Man, what a nightmare." His eyes were puffy and one side of his face was wrinkled from where he had rested his head on the side of his arms.

"Wasn't a nightmare, buddy," Joe said. "We really fought a giant werewolf and then a giant bat."

Bob rubbed the back of his head. "No. I don't mean that. I mean my dream. I dreamt I was being attacked by some Amazon woman who kept beating my head onto the floor."

Nina stifled a laugh.

"Yeah, well," Joe said, taking the last bite of his toast, "I don't want to get into any of *your* dreams. Reality is scary enough."

Joe sighed and touched the side of his head. "Oww," he said softly. The lump left by Angela's literature book had gone down, but the pain had not. He grabbed another piece of toast. "I'd like to know what you did to defeat Slice."

"Who knows with Lover Boy," Nina said with a shrug.

"What?" Bob said. He had dumped several ounces of jam and a glob of butter onto a slice of toast and spread it around. Then he crammed half of it into his mouth.

Nina smiled. "Who's *Mona*?"

Bob choked and almost spit out his toast.

"Not again!" Joe said as he jumped up and moved away from his friend. "You've already thrown up on me once. That's enough."

Nina cocked one eyebrow and took her glass to the sink. "Maybe I'll call Angela at the hospital," she said as she rinsed out her glass.

"She's not at the hospital," Bob said between mouthfuls.

"How do you know that? You were passed out, dreaming about Mona," Nina said.

"Because I saw her disappear in a mist before I passed out." Bob wiped his mouth with the back of his hand.

Nina shook her head. "What do you mean, she disappeared in a mist?"

"Joe got knocked out and just before I passed out, the giant bat turned into a red cloud, hovered over Angela and then, *poof*, she was gone."

Nina walked up to Bob and leaned her face close to his. "Don't you think that should have been the first thing you told us when you came in here?"

"I was hungry," Bob protested.

"Where is she?" Nina demanded.

"I don't know," Bob said.

"Well, what do you think happened?" Nina asked, frustrated.

Joe and Bob looked at each other and shrugged.

"The last thing I remember," Bob began, "is the vampire turning into a red cloud."

"Red cloud?" Nina said.

"Yeah," Bob said. He grabbed another piece of toast, splattered it with jam and butter, and shoved it in his mouth. "A giant red cloud. It just floated in the air, and then I just floated to sleep."

"You sure you didn't get hit in the head by something and just dream it?" Nina said, one eyebrow raised.

Bob stared back at Nina. "Did I hear you say something about being attacked by a giant bat?"

"From what Joe told me, it was at the same time you were being attacked by your fog and wolf," Nina said.

Bob punched Joe in the arm. "How come you left me lying on the floor?"

"How come you let me fight that werewolf myself?"

"Man, I had just been spun around like a top, and then that wolf head-butts me. Luckily, my projectile vomiting scared him away," Bob said.

"Ah, yes, your secret weapon — hurling," Joe replied sarcastically.

"Knock it off, you two. We've got to focus here," Nina said. "We've got to figure out what Slice was up to last night and why he was in Angela's room. Devin's his girlfriend."

"Maybe he got confused," Bob said. "You know he was in a fog."

Nina frowned at Bob. It was Joe's turn to punch Bob in the arm.

"That's pretty insensitive, Captain Boob," Joe said. "For all we know, he could have been trying to kill Angela."

Bob lowered his head and bit into more toast.

Nina stomped out of the kitchen.

"Where you going?" Joe said. He stood and followed her.

"To wake Devin," Nina replied to Joe. "She's got to know something. She's Slice's girlfriend."

"Oh, man," Bob said with a groan. "I need more food." But he jumped up and followed them.

"You think she's involved in her sister's kidnapping?" Joe asked as they climbed the stairs.

"Maybe she knew what Slice was up to," Bob suggested. "Maybe she had completed her transformation into a full-fledged vampire."

"But you said she tried to stop Slice with the cross," Nina pointed out.

"Oh, yeah," Joe said softly.

Nina pushed the door open. "Devin, you need to wake up."

Bob flipped on the light, and the kids entered the room.

It was empty.

Now Devin was gone, too.

CHAPTER SEVENTEEN
SATURDAY MORNING, 10:20 A.M.

"There she goes!" Bob yelled, looking out Devin's bedroom window. "She's leaving in her car."

They ran down the stairs and out the front door.

"Shotgun," Bob yelled as Nina jumped into the driver's seat.

Bob and Joe pushed and shoved each other, wrestling for the front seat.

"Just get in!" Nina yelled. "She's getting away!"

Joe put his arms around Bob, picked him up, threw him into the backseat, and hopped into the front.

"Someday I'm gonna —" Bob began, but he didn't get a chance to finish.

Nina fired up the engine, stomped on the accelerator, and the car catapulted forward, the tires squealing.

"Hey!" Bob bounced around in the backseat as the rear swung back and forth. Bob grabbed the armrest and steadied himself long enough to strap the seat belt across his waist.

"Where's she going?" Joe asked.

"I don't know." Nina could see the back of Devin's green Buick a half a mile ahead.

On a normal summer Saturday, the roads of San Tomas Inlet would be crowded with summer residents and tourists. But this was September and still early in the morning, so the traffic was light. Nina lifted her foot from the accelerator.

"What are you doing?" Bob said. "She's going to get away."

"I don't want to spook her," Nina replied.

"Spook her?" Bob said. "Spook someone who is one transfusion away from being counted among the living dead?"

"If she was that close to being a vampire," Joe interrupted, "would she be driving around in the daylight? And remember how she attacked Slice with the cross?"

"What?" Bob said, puzzled. He sat back into the seat. A moment later he said, "I think you've got something there, Joe my boy."

"She may not be completely under Slice's influence," Nina said, "but she knows what Slice is up to. Maybe she'll lead us to Slice and Angela."

"We need to stop to get a hammer, some stakes, and some silver bullets," Bob said.

"I thought silver bullets were just for werewolves," Joe said, turning in his seat to face Bob.

"I'm not taking any chances," Bob said.

"We're not getting any hammer, stakes, or silver bullets," Nina said. "We're going to find out where Slice has Angela and we're going to call Detective Turner."

"You think Detective Turner will believe us?" Joe said.

"I don't know," Nina replied. "He's your friend."

"He thinks those murders were committed by a serial killer with a blood lust," said Joe.

Nina watched Devin turn her car onto Beach Front Road.

"Where do you think she's going?" Joe asked.

Nina followed Devin's car. "I don't know."

They continued driving in silence.

Nina had always thought of herself as sensible, logical, and not given to too many flights of fancy. She liked a good story, especially a good horror story, but she knew the difference between reality and fantasy. Now her neat little world and its neat little division into reality and fantasy had been shattered. Three days earlier, she would have laughed at Captain Bob and Joe and their overactive, immature imaginations. Today she was following someone who may or may not have been a vampire, in search of another person who *was* a vampire, hoping to find her best friend before *she* could be turned into a vampire.

And all because they had wanted to watch classic horror movies on a defective, experimental projector they had no business messing with in the first place.

Nina slowed the car as they approached a large abandoned building.

"This is unreal," Bob exclaimed from the back-seat.

"I'd forgotten all about this place," Joe added.

Nina watched Devin steer her car into the driveway of a vacant resort hotel. She, too, had forgotten about the dilapidated hotel on the north edge of San Tomas Inlet.

Sixty years earlier, the hotel had been the small town's number-one attraction. Movie stars, famous authors, politicians, and wealthy landowners had made the hotel their summer getaway. Over the years, the dominance of this large, opulent hotel gave way to smaller motel chains that offered cheap rooms right on the beach. But even in its dying days, the hotel was known as the "Ritz of the South." Its real name was the Carfax Hotel.

Nina slowly drove by the entrance to the abandoned hotel. They all watched as Devin's car stopped. She jumped out of her car and ran into the ten-story building through a gaping hole that once had been covered by large, carved doors.

"Now what?" Bob said.

"You need to call your friend, Detective Turner," Nina said to Joe.

"I don't know if he'll believe us," Joe said.

"I don't think it's a good idea," Bob said.

"Why not?" Nina said, looking back at Bob.

"Like Joe said," Bob began, "he wouldn't believe us, for one thing."

"And?"

"And what?"

"You said *for one thing*. What's the other thing?"

"Oh," Bob said. He adjusted his yacht captain's hat. "For another thing, *we* made this mess. *We've* got to clean it up."

"He's right," Joe said. "Detective Turner will think we're crazy. *I* think we're crazy, now that I think about it."

Nina sighed. "Okay. I'm just trying to keep you two out of as much trouble as possible." The car moved forward slowly.

"You're not my mother," Bob protested.

"If I were your mother, I'd have you confined to a padded room," Nina shot back.

"If you were my mother, I'd confine *myself* to a padded room."

"*Freshmen*," Nina said under her breath.

"I heard that."

"You were *meant* to hear it!"

They sat in silence.

Nina stared straight ahead, her mind racing. *What are we walking into? A vampire's den? Slice has become the walking twenty-first century version of Count Dracula. He can transform himself into a mist, a bat, a werewolf, and giant ticks. How can three inexperienced teenagers stop him?*

Bob broke the silence. "Now what?"

"We wait," Nina said.

"I say we go in, find Devin, and find out what she knows," Bob said.

"I don't know —" Nina began.

Bob ignored Nina. "What do you say, Joe?"

"I say," Joe began, "that we help Devin." Joe opened the door, jumped from the car, and ran up the stairs of the old hotel. He stopped short at the front door.

Back in the car, Nina and Bob looked at each other. Then they both opened their car doors and ran after their friend.

Joe stood in the doorway, peering inside.

"What's wrong?" Bob said.

Devin lay just beyond the threshold, a trickle of blood at the corner of her mouth.

CHAPTER EIGHTEEN

Joe's first instinct was to rush to Devin, to help her, to pull her out of danger. Every muscle in his body was tensed to spring into action. However, something at the back of his mind told him to take things slowly.

Devin looked helpless and unconscious. But she also looked like a trap for the teens.

"What are we waiting for?" Bob said. He started inside. Joe stopped him.

"Just wait," Joe cautioned. "Let me go first. No sense in all of us getting trapped."

Joe walked softly to Devin. He looked around and then down at her motionless form. He knelt and felt her wrist. "Devin," he said softly. She moaned. She had a pulse, but it was faint. She had grown pale again. Joe pulled back her upper lip. Devin's canine teeth had grown. She was reverting back into a vampire.

"Is she alive?" Bob called from the doorway.

"Barely," Joe replied. He signaled them to join

him. "It's clear. But look at this." He pointed to her teeth.

"Man," Bob said. "Is it possible for the undead to become un-undead and then become un-un-undead again?"

"Apparently," Joe said.

"This will stop her undeadness," Bob said. He knelt down next to the sleeping Devin and placed several strings of garlic around her, outlining her body.

"Kind of ironic," Joe said.

"What?" Nina said.

"With the garlic around her, she looks like one of those chalk outlines detectives make at the scene of a homicide."

"Let's hope not," Nina said.

A strand of garlic hit against Devin's arm. Her mouth opened and she hissed, but she didn't wake up.

"Why do you think she began to revert back?" Nina said.

"The cross and garlic must have started to return Devin to normal," Bob said. "But if this is Slice's lair, then she must be succumbing to his evil influence."

"I really want all of us to get out of here!" Nina said. Strain showed on her face, and she fought back tears.

Bob swallowed. "I was just trying to explain a possible reason."

"I know. I just want to know what we need to do to help Angela and save Devin," Nina said.

"Then let's get Devin out of here," Joe suggested.

"Shouldn't we call Detective Turner?" Bob said.

"I thought you were gung ho to hunt vampires and drive stakes through their hearts," Nina fired back.

"Look, I've seen this guy change into a wolf, then he changed into a fog that spun me like a top, and then he changed into a giant bat." Bob pointed at Devin. "He's got enough power to turn her back into one of his minions just by being near her. We have no hammer; we have no stakes; and this garlic is only good enough to keep him at arm's length!" Bob was visibly shaken. "And my arms are pretty darn short!"

"This is a pretty big place," Joe said. "I don't see how we can cover it all by ourselves. We should call Detective Turner."

"We can't call him now," Nina said, tension in her voice. "First we have to get Devin out of here."

Bob blurted out. "There must be over one hundred rooms, not to mention the basement and storage rooms. We're going to need help finding Slice."

"Aren't you scared?" Nina asked.

Bob was silent for several moments. He bit his bottom lip.

"Aren't we all?" Joe finally said.

"Help me lift her up," Bob said, kneeling down.

They carried Devin to Nina's car and gently placed her in the backseat.

A dark car pulled into the entryway of the old hotel.

"Who's that?" Nina said.

"Hey!" Bob said slowly. "That's Abel's car."

The car stopped alongside Nina's. Abel hopped out. "Hey, guys. What's up?"

"Chasing vampires," Bob said.

"Really?" Abel said, a slight smile on his lips.

"What are you doing here?" Nina said.

"I was driving by and I saw your car. Thought maybe you were having car trouble and wanted to help."

"How do you know my car?"

"It's hard to miss a fine machine like yours," he said with a smile. Nina smiled and blushed. Devin was right: Abel was charming. "I've also noticed it outside of Devin's house the last couple of nights. You're Nina, right? Devin told me you were spending the weekend with her and Angela."

"Speaking of Devin," Bob said. "She's in the back. Sleeping."

Abel walked over to the car and looked inside. Concern covered his face. "Is she all right?"

"I don't know," Nina said. "She left the house and we followed her here."

"Why did you follow her? And why would she come here?"

Joe ignored the first question and answered the

second. "We haven't figured that out yet. She was just inside the doorway there."

Bob blurted, "She's become a vampire again."

"What? Really?" Abel opened the car door and leaned inside to examine Devin more closely. "She was feeling okay when I left her the other night. Told her to take last night off and get some rest. Had to chase Slice away from the house."

"Slice was at the house the night before last?" Nina asked.

"Yeah. I don't know how he got inside, but when I found him, he was trying to bite Devin's neck."

"What were you doing in the house?" Nina said suspiciously.

Abel backed out of the car and leaned against it. "After I dropped Devin off, I saw Slice's car sitting just around the corner. I doubled back and heard them arguing inside, but the front door was locked. So, I sneaked around until I found the back door open. I stopped Slice just before he could bite her."

Nina looked at Abel. Instinctively, her suspicions were aroused; however, something about the handsome young man washed her fears away. She didn't know if it was his smile, his well-groomed hair, or his eyes — the dark, deep eyes that seemed so open and honest.

Abel met Nina's gaze. "Why don't you boys help me get Devin into my car? I'll take her back home and call a friend of mine who's a doctor."

"You think it's okay to move her?" Nina asked.

"Hey, I'm a doctor, aren't I?"

"Actually, you're a dentist," Captain Bob said.

"Yeah, but I went to medical school first, then dropped out to be a dentist. I still remember some of my training. Devin needs to be looked at by someone who actually completed medical school. And then she needs to get home in her own bed and rest. Okay?"

Nina hesitated for a moment. "Sure, Abel. That sounds great." She turned to Joe and Bob. "Can you two put Devin in his car?"

Bob and Joe nodded and went to get Devin. They gently lifted her and arranged her as comfortably as they could in the backseat of Abel's car.

"Call me if you need any help," Abel said as he climbed into the driver's seat. He sped away.

Nina watched Abel's car as it disappeared down the driveway.

"Hello, Earth to Nina, hello," said Bob, waving his hands in front of Nina's face.

"What?" Nina said, confused. "What? What are you talking about?"

Bob and Joe laughed.

"If your eyes weren't firmly attached to their sockets, they would have fallen out and followed Abel all the way back to Devin's house," Joe quipped.

Nina shook her head. "Don't be silly."

"Don't change the subject," Joe said, nudging

Bob in the side. "You can't fool us. You've got the hots for Dr. Molar."

"Oh, shut up," Nina said with a groan. She grinned despite herself. "Come on, this is serious. Now Devin's safe, but I'm worried about Angela. She's been gone for hours, and who knows what Slice has done to her?"

Joe was about to agree when a scream echoed from the deserted hotel.

CHAPTER NINETEEN

The trio stood frozen and silent until the scream died away.

Nina was the first to speak. "What now?"

"That could be Angela," Joe said. "I say we go in and get her."

"Good plan, buddy," Bob said. "You're forgetting one thing."

"What's that?"

"If Slice is Dracula, and he's in there with Angela, we're going to need more than our wits and some strands of garlic."

"Like what?" Nina said.

"Like real vampire-killing equipment. I say we go get some."

Joe and Nina nodded in silent agreement. They climbed back into Nina's car.

"One thing I can't figure out," Nina said, still in a whisper, as they headed down the long, broken driveway, "is why Slice went after Angela. Devin's his girlfriend."

"I don't know," Bob responded. "Maybe to lure Devin to the hotel?"

"But why bother going to those lengths when he could have just taken Devin that night?" Joe asked.

Bob frowned. "I don't know."

Two hours later, the trio stood once more at the broad entrance of the dilapidated Carfax Hotel, each ready for the battle ahead. Nina held a large silver cross she had borrowed from her grandmother. She also had a strong flashlight. Joe had a handful of tent stakes in his left hand and a small mallet in his right. Bob had strings of garlic around his neck and a bag full of Communion wafers. He'd insisted on stopping at a church, where he was able to sneak in through a side door and grab the bag of Communion wafers. He would debate the ethics and irony of stealing Communion wafers to fight the Prince of Darkness later.

They had seen *Dracula* enough times to know that the vampire would have to rest in darkness during the day to order to restore his unnatural supernatural powers. Sunlight wouldn't kill a vampire, but it would sap his strength, leaving him weak and vulnerable. So Nina, Joe, and Bob had decided to start their search in the darkest place of all — the hotel basement.

They made their way through the kitchen and the service entrance and found the wide staircase leading down to the basement. None of them had ever been in the old hotel and really didn't know what they would find. But they had prepared themselves as best they could.

The basement was a labyrinth of passages that led to large storage rooms, each a potential hiding place for Slice and his hostage. They entered each room with caution and fear. Nina directed the flashlight this way and that, and Joe held the hammer and stake ready. Bob swung the ropes of garlic like a pendulum, ready to fire the strands of the aromatic, anti-vampire vegetable at anything that remotely resembled a blood-sucking monster. They spoke softly so their voices wouldn't echo throughout the basement corridors.

"Doesn't appear to be in B-1," Joe said.

"How many basement floors are there?" Bob said.

"I don't know," Nina replied.

"Does it feel cold down here to you guys?" Bob said.

"I don't know," Joe said. "I'm shivering too much from fear."

"Yeah," Nina agreed. She pointed the flashlight to a large opening. "Here's the stairs to the second basement floor." She turned to the two boys, her flashlight illuminating them.

"Hey!" Bob raised his hands to block the light as if it blinded him.

"When we find Slice, we destroy him," Nina said with firmness.

"Of course," Bob said. He started off down the stairs. Nina grabbed his arm.

"But we don't kill Angela. Even if she's already a vampire."

The light hit Bob from underneath, casting an eerie pallor over his face. "We find what we find," he said.

"We take Angela out of here and try to cure her," Nina said.

"She's right," Joe said. "Angela's a friend. Maybe when we destroy Slice, Angela will be okay."

"Let's hope so," Bob said.

They walked side by side down the stairs. When they reached the bottom, Nina pointed the flashlight first to the right, then to the left.

"Which way, guys?" Nina asked.

"Left," Bob said.

"Fine with me," Joe replied.

They had only gone a few steps when a soft noise startled them.

"What was that?" Joe whispered.

"Whatever it was," Bob said slowly, every hair on the back on his neck standing on end, "it came from behind us."

They all turned simultaneously and began walking in the opposite direction.

Nina held the flashlight shoulder high, the beam bathing everything in front of them in a bright white light.

A low, soft moan echoed throughout the hallway.

"It's coming from one of those rooms," Nina said, pointing the flashlight to her right.

"Is the vampire behind door Number One, door Number Two, or door Number Three?" Bob asked in his best game-show-host voice.

"Let's start with door Number One," Joe suggested. He moved to the side of the door and placed his hand on it. "It's cold." He looked at Nina. "I'll push it open. Bob, you ready?"

"Yeah," Bob replied. He held the strings of garlic high, like a cowboy ready to lasso a bull.

"Here goes." Joe pushed on the door, and it swung open easily.

Nina stepped forward, pointing the flashlight into the room. It was empty.

Joe moved to the second door, and they repeated the process. It was empty as well, except for several lumps of canvas scattered about.

But suddenly, a high-pitched screech filled the room. Luminous yellow eyes stared angrily at the trio.

Joe raised the hammer and stake, ready to strike. Bob twirled the garlic over his head.

"Wait!" Nina shouted. "It's only a cat."

The cat hissed. Its ears were pinned back, the fur on its back and neck standing up straight. It looked the teens up and down, then shot out between Joe and Bob.

"Whoa!" Bob said as he dodged the frightened cat. "That can't be good luck."

"Well," Joe said. "There goes the element of surprise."

"Yeah," Nina agreed.

"All right, Slice," Bob began, "if you're down here, then you know that we're in here, too." Joe and Nina looked at each other and frowned. "All we want is Angela, and then you can go back to your undead nightmares. Okay?" Bob kicked at a lump of canvas.

"Has he gone insane?" Nina said to Joe.

"No," Joe replied. "But I think he just registered a 7.6 on the crazy scale."

Bob kicked at a second lump of canvas. It flew straight into the air.

"Oh, my God!" Nina cried. She almost dropped the flashlight.

Lying under the canvas was a body covered by dozens of enormous ticks. Their heads were burrowed through the figure's clothing and into his skin. The bodies pulsed as they sucked blood from the figure's lifeless form. But then the head raised itself slightly from the floor.

"Help . . . me," came a weak voice, and then a gurgling sound.

"Slice?" Bob said.

"Slice?" Nina exclaimed.

"Slice," Joe confirmed.

"Help me," came the same gurgling moan. Then Slice's head fell back to the floor.

The ticks were either unaware of the three teens, or just chose to ignore them. Either way, the blood-engorged ticks continued their feast on Slice's already-emaciated body.

CHAPTER TWENTY
SATURDAY, 2:30 P.M.

"I hate bugs!" Bob yelled. He whipped at the ticks with a strand of garlic. Tiny squeals of pain filled the room.

"I didn't know bugs could scream," Joe said.

"These are unholy bugs of the dead!" Bob shouted as he continued whipping them. "And I hate them more than any other kind of bug."

Several ticks pulled away from Slice. They rose up to face Bob, spitting blood at their attacker.

Bob yelled and moved back. More ticks jumped from Slice's body and made for Bob.

Joe fell to his knees and began striking at the two-inch ticks with his hammer. Each time he hit one, it exploded with a scream and a splatter of blood.

"Let's get out of here!" Nina screamed.

A voice exploded in the room. "No one's going anywhere!"

Stunned, the trio froze in place.

As if by some silent command, the ticks embedded in Slice and the ticks attacking Bob stopped. They scrambled toward one another and began piling up on top of each other. Nina, Joe, and Bob watched in amazement and horror as the black, blood-engorged ticks stacked themselves higher and higher.

"Look," Bob said as he pointed at the bottom of the pile.

The ticks began to change form, to flatten out and lose their roundness. They were losing their individuality and merging together, as if some invisible sculptor were molding clay. The transformation started near the floor and inched slowly upward as the form of a man appeared.

The shoulders, neck, and head were the last to transform. With a hiss and a sigh, the face took shape. It shook back and forth in a fluid, blurring motion.

When it stopped, Nina, Joe, and Bob were staring into the luminous eyes of Abel Dunn.

"The dentist?" Bob shouted. "You're the vampire? You're the Prince of Darkness? You're Dracula? We thought Slice was —"

"Slice," the vampire hissed, "was a servant." He turned toward the near-lifeless Goth band leader. "A poor foolish servant."

"Where's Angela? Where's Devin?" Nina demanded.

"You wish to join them?" the vampire said, his eyes flashing at Nina.

"I wish to destroy you," Nina said through clenched teeth.

The vampire growled, opening his mouth wide to reveal long, sharp teeth.

"Those teeth look really terrible. You should see a dentist, Dunn," Bob said.

"My name is not Dunn. My name is Dracula!"

As he spoke, a second transformation took place. The dark, suave looks of Abel Dunn gave way to the dark, suave looks of Dracula — ancient burial tux, black cape, black shiny hair combed back from a prominent widow's peak. *The* Count Dracula that had struck terror into moviegoers seventy years earlier now stood before them in the flesh.

This wasn't a movie. This was reality. But Joe had learned from the movies what to do when confronted by a monster.

He lunged at the vampire. He shoved Dracula against the wall and placed the stake in the middle of his chest. He pulled back his right arm, his hand clenching the hammer.

As quick as lightning, Dracula grabbed Joe's right wrist and twisted his arm downward. Joe screamed in pain and dropped the hammer. He pushed on the stake, trying to drive the wooden shard in by using sheer force.

Dracula grimaced in pain. He grabbed Joe's

wrist and slowly pushed the stake away from his chest. In a flash, Joe found himself with his back against the wall and the stake pressed against the middle of his own heart.

"How do you like your stake?" Dracula said with a smirk. Even his voice had changed. Gone was the smooth, natural voice Abel had used to befriend them all. In its place was a rich and deadly Hungarian accent, slow and menacing. "Raw, medium, or well done?" He leaned on the stake, gradually pushing it against Joe's chest.

"Let go of my friend, coffin breath!" Bob shouted. He looped a strand of garlic around the vampire's neck and pulled him backward.

The vampire screamed as the garlic burned into his throat. He dropped the stake and grabbed for the garlic. Bob pulled back with all his strength and jerked him away from Joe. Joe fell to the floor, clutching his chest.

Bob tightened the garlic noose. Dracula was a head taller than him, but Bob had the advantage. He hung on to two ends of the garlic strand and let himself dangle an inch or two above the floor, putting all his weight against the vampire's. He didn't know if it was possible to strangle the undead. All he could do was try.

But unexpectedly, Bob hit the floor with his knees. Dracula had transformed into a mist and floated away.

"There!" Nina shouted, pointing at the mist as it hovered near the ceiling.

"You okay?" Joe asked as he helped Bob stand up.

"I need steel kneecaps," Bob replied, groaning.

By the time they looked at the ceiling, Dracula had transformed himself back into the giant half human, half bat that had attacked them the night before.

"Hey!" Bob shouted up. "Why don't you come down and fight like a man?"

Dracula swooped down at Nina. She ducked and swung the flashlight at the diving vampire. Dracula reached for her, his razor-sharp claws scratching her arm. Nina screamed in pain.

Dracula swooped back to the ceiling. Nina knelt on the floor, holding her arm.

Bob had seen enough. He grabbed the hammer and the stake.

"Hey, Dracula," he shouted up at the vampire. "Why don't you pick on someone your own size?"

The vampire looked down at Bob with a blank stare.

"Yeah, I'm talking to you, you flying bag of pestilence." Bob took a step forward. "Chicken? Yeah. You don't look like a big, scary vampire bat. You look like a chicken. A chicken that's been plucked and is ready for the oven. Come down here, chicken." Bob made loud clucking sounds.

Dracula's face twisted into anger. He flapped his wings, sending a cold wind down on his challenger.

Bob continued clucking. "What are you afraid of, you big chicken?"

Dracula swooped down toward Bob. Bob waited until the vampire was nearly upon him before falling to his knees and raising the stake over his head.

Dracula screamed as the stake tore through his right wing. Bob spun around just in time to see him tilt back and forth, out of control, and then slam into the far wall. The vampire fell to the floor in a crumpled heap.

"Now!" Bob shouted at Joe as he ran to the fallen figure of the vampire. Bob grabbed Dracula by the shoulder and spun him around.

The vampire hissed and struck Bob across the face. Bob slumped to the floor, stunned. Dracula transformed himself back into human, but Joe was on him before he could escape.

Joe pounced on the vampire's chest. "Give me the hammer!" He pinned the vampire to the floor, grabbing him by the throat. He began choking the vampire for all he was worth.

Dracula struggled, but he seemed weakened to Joe. The vampire grabbed Joe's wrists, but Joe's anger and determination gave him extra strength. The vampire could not break free of the teenager's hold.

Bob placed the stake over the vampire's heart

and Joe brought the hammer down with such force that the stake went through the body and thunked against the concrete basement floor.

Dracula screamed and grabbed at the stake.

"No blood!" Bob shouted.

Bob was right. Instead, a gray liquid slowly oozed from around the stake. Then the stake melted and was absorbed into the wound, which sealed up with a quick sucking sound.

Dracula smiled. "You cannot kill me, my weak, mortal friends," he said in a thick Hungarian accent. "I am not of this world."

Dracula sat up, brushing Joe back effortlessly. The vampire got to his feet and looked down at the two boys. An evil smile stretched across his face. "And if you'll excuse me, I must find my bride, my beautiful *Mina*."

"I've had enough of this!" Nina shouted. She ran at Dracula and swung a two-by-four at him. Dracula turned in time to catch the brunt of the blow on the side of his head.

The vampire went down, an ugly gash running the length of his head.

A moment later he rose. The teens watched in horror as the gash closed itself and healed instantly.

"You will not be able to destroy me," he said, his deep accent echoing off the concrete walls. "I am not of this world. You brought me here, and in doing so have given me powers that I could not imagine in my old world. For this, I thank you." The evil smile spread across his face, and he bowed like a genteel European gentleman.

Then he raised the sides of his cape, transformed into a bat, and flew up and out of the basement.

CHAPTER TWENTY-ONE
TEN MINUTES LATER

"Don't worry about the seats!" Nina shouted as they ran out of the old hotel.

Just behind her were Joe and Bob. The two boys were carrying the wan and near-lifeless body of Slice.

Nina pulled her cell phone from her back pocket. She punched 911 and jumped into the driver's seat, pushing the passenger seat forward so Joe and Bob could lay Slice down in the back. Joe hopped into the front.

"You're not leaving me back here with this guy," Bob said, hopping out of the car. "He could be a vampire!"

"What?" Joe fired back. "You want to ride on my lap?"

Bob thought for a moment. Then he decided he'd rather take his chances with a potential vampire than be seen riding around town on Joe's lap. He carefully crawled into the back, holding a strand of garlic in front him.

"Yeah!" Nina shouted into the phone. "He's hurt badly. We're taking him to the hospital . . . No! We can't wait for an ambulance . . . Tell Detective Turner to meet us at the hospital." She flipped the phone up and fired up the engine. The tires squealed as they careened down the driveway.

Moments later, they were pulling into the emergency entrance of San Tomas Inlet Hospital. Two paramedics with a gurney were waiting. One climbed in the back just as Bob climbed out. The paramedic flashed a penlight into Slice's eyes.

"Fixed and dilated!" she shouted. "Got to move him, stat."

The male paramedic reached over the edge of the car and helped her lift Slice out of the car and onto the gurney. A nurse joined them. The head paramedic shouted her orders as they rushed the gurney in through the emergency room doors.

"You want to tell me what this is all about?" Detective Turner said as he walked up to the trio. He was wearing a trench coat over jeans and a wrinkled pajama top. Red plaid slippers were on his feet. His thinning hair was pointing in every direction.

"Catch you during your beauty sleep?" Bob said with a smile. "What are you doing sleeping in the middle of the afternoon?"

"I had a stakeout until nine this morning, okay?"

"Love the slippers," Bob commented.

"Just tell me what's going on," Turner said.

"We found Slice," Nina said. "We thought he was the vampire, but it's really Dr. Dunn."

"The dentist?" the detective asked.

"Yeah," Bob said. "No, I mean, he's not really Dr. Dunn. He's really Dracula. You know, from the movie."

"What movie?" Turner said.

"You know," Bob said, exasperated. *"Dracula!* The movie."

Detective Turner looked at Bob. Then he looked at Joe and Nina. He was silent for a moment, then said to Nina, "You know, I expect this from those two. But you? I don't know you that well, but I had the impression you were the brains of the outfit."

"Well, I —" Nina began.

"What's the problem?" Bob shouted. "We told you what happened. Dr. Dunn is really Count Dracula. *The* Count Dracula! Transylvania! Carfax Abbey! Vampire! Werewolf! Bats!"

"All right!" Detective Turner said, putting a hand on Bob's shoulder. "Calm down."

Bob was huffing. Sweat poured down his brow.

"I know it sounds crazy," Nina said. She tried to laugh, but failed. "I thought they were crazy too. But I saw it."

"You saw what?" Turner ran his fingers through his thinning hair.

"I saw Dr. Dunn change into Dracula. Just like in the movie."

"You *think* you saw it."

"No. I saw it," Nina declared positively.

Turner sighed. "Dispatch said you found Slice in the basement of the old Carfax Hotel, right?"

"Yes."

"That place is dark; kinda spooky."

"Yeah."

"You went looking for vampires."

"No," Nina interrupted. "We went looking for our friends. Angela and Devin."

Turner scowled at Bob. "You went into a spooky old hotel, down into the basement with vampires and monsters on your minds, and you found Slice and Dr. Dunn. You just think you saw Dr. Dunn change into a giant bat." He shook his head. "Look, maybe Dr. Dunn is involved with this vampire cult we're looking for. Maybe Slice is one of his victims or maybe he's a member. We don't know. But we'll check into it. Okay?"

"Great!" Nina said.

"*Tomorrow*." Turner started heading for his unmarked police car.

"What?" Nina asked, stunned.

"I said, tomorrow." Turner turned up the collar of his trench coat.

"What about our friends?" Nina cried.

"Your friends?" Turner smiled. "I called the Chavarria home on the way over here. Devin said that Angela was there and she was getting dinner ready."

"What? She must be under the vampire's spell again," Nina muttered.

Turner just stared at her and shook his head. "No kidnapping. No vampires. Nothing that goes bump in the night. There's no electricity in that building. By the time I can get an investigative team together, it'll be too dark. I'm not going to traipse around there tonight. Tomorrow morning I'll round up a couple of officers and we'll look it over."

"But —"

Turner raised his hands. "You'll have to settle for that. Tomorrow. When it's light. Now, you kids go home and get some sleep. I'll call you if we find anything. *Tomorrow*." He sighed and walked away, climbing into his car. "Go home," he repeated. Then he drove off.

"That's just great," Nina said, throwing her hands into the air. "He thinks this is all some sort of mass hallucination. I thought you guys said he was your friend," Nina said. She stomped toward her car.

"He is," Joe said. "He just doesn't believe us."

"Now what?" Bob said.

"We return to the hotel and find Angela," Nina said as she started the engine.

"Wait a minute!" Bob said. He stood by the driver's side, looking down at Nina. "Within the last twenty-four hours, I've had to fight bats and were-wolves and red mists and ticks. Less than an hour ago, I almost had my throat ripped apart by a vampire from a movie made over seventy years ago! I'm not anxious to run over there so quickly. I say we go back tomorrow when we have more daylight."

Nina stared forward. "I'll tell you what, *Captain Bob*: you just go home. Make yourself one of those disgusting peanut butter and hot dog sandwiches, lie down on your couch and play finger tag with your remote control." She turned and stared up at Bob, her brown eyes cold and hard. "I'm going back to the Carfax Hotel to find my friend." She started the car, the engine roaring as she pressed on the accelerator.

"You think I'm a coward?" Bob hollered above the metallic thunder.

"I think you've got enough hot air to raise the *Titanic*."

Bob's nostrils flared and his eyes widened. "I'll tell you something about hot air —"

"Hey!" Joe shouted. "This isn't helping Angela or Devin!" He took a breath. He looked at Bob. "We can't wait until tomorrow. You saw what Dracula can do. Tomorrow may be too late."

Bob continued to glare down at Nina. His breathing was short and hot. He glanced up at Joe. "I'm not a coward," he said softly.

"No. You're not," Joe replied. "You're just like Nina and me. Scared. That's all. But we can't wait. Okay? We've got to go back tonight. But first we've got to make a plan, or we're just gonna get our butts kicked like we did this afternoon. Agreed?"

Bob took a deep breath. He looked down at Nina. Her face had softened. A glint of light flashed from her eyes. Bob realized that she was holding back tears.

He adjusted his hat. "Agreed. And it's *bologna*. Not hot dogs," he said. "Only a barbarian would eat peanut butter and hot dogs." He climbed into the backseat.

Nina took a deep breath. "Agreed." She shifted the transmission into drive and pulled out slowly.

The red sun lingered on the horizon. Sweethearts would have welcomed such a sunset during the summer; however, during the oncoming chill of fall, the red sun carried a warning: Red sky at night — horror's delight.

CHAPTER TWENTY-TWO
6:16 P.M.

Nina, Joe, and Bob sat silently for several moments in Bob's living room. They had spent the better part of the last hour trying to formulate a plan.

"We've been overlooking something," Bob said.

"What?" Joe said.

Bob shrugged his shoulders. "I don't know. That's what I mean. We've been overlooking something. There's something we haven't figured out yet."

Nina sat on the couch. Joe sat on a bar stool at the counter that separated the kitchen-dining room from the living room. Bob was sitting at his computer desk. He looked at Nina. Her head was bowed.

"Nina?" She didn't look up. "Dracula said he wasn't of this world. That means he knows he's from the movie. For some reason the traditional ways of killing him won't work. We drove a stake through his heart and you about took his head off with that board, but he was instantly healed. He just laughed at us. What did he say? He's looking for his bride? What bride?"

"Remember," Joe began, "in the movie Count Dracula leaves Transylvania to live in London because he's looking for a large city with fresh blood. Then he sees Mina Seward and falls in love with her, believing that she is the long-lost love he has sought throughout eternity."

"And Devin is his 'Mina' in this world," Bob added. "She's been in league with him all along."

Nina sighed and looked up. "That makes sense, Bob. That makes a lot of sense."

Joe shook his head. "It's our fault all of this has happened."

"And we're the only ones who understand what is really happening here," Nina said. "We've tried to explain this, and everyone thinks we're crazy —"

"Or just a bunch of stupid kids," Bob said. "We don't even know if Dracula is real or not."

"What do you mean?" Nina said.

"Is Dracula real? We know he is the Dracula who has escaped from the movie," Bob explained. "But, is he a real person who has been possessed by the fictionalized Dracula, or is he the real Dracula in a modern disguise? We can't kill him in the tried-and-true way of killing vampires. We've tried that."

"I'm open to suggestions," Joe said.

"He kept saying he's not of this world," Bob said, talking more to himself than to his friends. "He's not of this world. But he's in our world. The laws of his world don't apply to him. Driving a stake through a vampire's heart or chopping off a vampire's head will kill a bloodsucker in the movies and the myths, but not in the real world. So, what will kill him in our world?"

"Remember what you said the other day: Maybe while we're watching the characters in a movie, they're actually watching us from their reality?" Joe said.

Nina remained silent, listening, letting the boys do their thinking out loud. She had an inkling where this train of thought was heading, but she knew that putting in her two cents worth might throw them off track.

"I was just showing off," Bob said.

"I know, but I think you may have been onto something," Joe said. "Okay, we released Count Dracula from a make-believe movie world into the real world. The rules about monsters and how to kill them only apply in their make-believe world —"

Bob jumped up. "And the only way to get rid of them is not to kill them, but to send them back into the make-believe world!" He turned to Nina. "You have a camcorder?"

"My parents do. Why?"

"The only way to kill Count Dracula is to send him back into his movie. To do that we've got to capture him on film and transfer him back into his movie."

"Like a vacuum camera," Joe said, his voice rising. "Instead of just recording images, we need a camera that will suck in the image, imprison it on tape."

"Yeah," Bob said, grinning. "That's why we need your camera. Joe's program for the projector can be reversed so that instead of sending out an image, it captures an image." Bob blinked, and his face dropped. "At least, I hope it will."

"I guess we're going to have to find out," Nina said. She got up and stepped toward the door.

Bob and Joe began to follow. But Nina suddenly stopped short, causing Bob and Joe to bump into each other. She turned and looked Bob in the eye. "You know, you can be pretty intelligent when you want to be. Sometimes, in moments like this, Captain Bob, I actually think there's hope for you yet." Then she turned, opened the door, and walked briskly out of the room. Joe followed her.

Bob stood in the middle of the room, stunned, his mouth hanging open.

Joe popped his head back in the door. "Come on, Captain Bob. Your destiny awaits you." He disappeared.

"I'm off, said the madman," Bob said quietly, smiling. Then he followed his friends.

CHAPTER TWENTY-THREE
13 SECONDS AFTER MIDNIGHT

Nina, Joe, and Bob stood in the broad entrance of the dilapidated Carfax Hotel, each armed with vampire-fighting gear.

Joe had added one more weapon to his arsenal of hammer and stakes. Strapped to his hip like a six-shooter from an old Western movie was the modified camcorder Nina had borrowed from her parents' home. The digital camera was the latest in electronic "must haves," and operated from a microprocessor and miniature RAM sticks, just like a computer. Joe was able to compress the 3-D program so it would fit on the camera's small ten-gig hard drive.

"Now tell me why we need these things?" Nina said, indicating the hammer, stakes, garlic, Communion wafers, and cross they'd brought with them. "You guys said he couldn't be killed this way."

"That's right," Joe said. "But he still reacts to them. They'll slow him down. I don't know how close I need to get to him with this camera, or how long it needs to run before he's absorbed."

"Oh, yeah," Nina said.

"There's something else," Joe added.

"I don't like the sound of that," Nina said.

"While you guys were getting more of the traditional stuff and I was transferring the program to the camera's disk, I watched the Dracula movie. We've been wrong about one very important thing."

"I *really* don't like the sound of that," Nina said.

"It's not Devin who Count Dracula thinks is his long-lost love, it's Angela," Joe said. "Angela could be Mina Seward's twin sister. He must have been using Devin to get to Angela."

"Well, that explains a lot," Nina said. She wrinkled her nose. "Eww. First he nearly kills her boyfriend, then her sister — and now he's in love with her. Poor girl." Nina took a deep breath. "Okay, ready."

"Ready," the boys said simultaneously.

Silently, they walked into the immense lobby of the dilapidated Carfax Hotel and toward the expansive staircase that led to the mezzanine. Dracula was immortal, undead, and intelligent. He wouldn't hide in the basement again. Joe had suggested they look for large linen closets. These had no windows, so they'd be perfect for creatures of the night who needed to avoid direct contact with the sun.

It was almost pitch-black inside the hotel. An occasional shaft of cold moonlight lit the stairs, sending strange shadows darting across the walls. The old building creaked and groaned as it settled for the night. But every sound, every shadow set the teens further on edge.

"Nina, are you sure we have to do this now? It can't wait till daylight?" Bob asked nervously.

"No. It has to be now. If we wait till tomorrow, Angela and Devin could be dead — or worse," Nina answered, a note of determination in her voice. "We have to do this. We released this monster, and only we know how to capture him again. I'm not going to let my friends die."

From the mezzanine they took the stairs to the third floor. Nina turned on her flashlight as they entered the main hallway. It was littered with debris and broken doors. The carpet was ripped and a musty smell hung in the air. They moved slowly, checking each room as they passed. They didn't speak. Instead, they listened — listened for any noise, natural or unnatural.

"Here's one," Joe said. He brushed dust from the metal sign on the door, revealing the word "Housekeeping" in art deco lettering. Joe pushed on the door, and it opened easily. He stepped back, holding up one of the stakes and the hammer. Nina thrust the light into the room.

Dust-covered sheets littered the floor. Shelves were knocked over and bottles of cleaning fluid were strewn here and there.

Nina, Joe, and Bob kicked the sheets about, but found nothing. They left the room and climbed the steps to the fourth floor. The fourth and fifth floors were empty as well. So were the sixth, seventh, and eighth.

"Maybe we're wrong," Nina said. "Maybe he's not here at all. Maybe he's hiding someplace else."

"Possibly," Bob said. "We'll know in a few minutes anyway."

"You're not building a lot of confidence in me," Nina said.

"Here, maybe this will help." Bob reached into his jeans pocket and pulled out a small bottle of water. He handed it to Nina.

"What is this?" Nina said, taking it.

"Holy water. It was sitting next to the Communion wafers. We can use all the help we can get."

Nina sighed and shook her head. "Shall we?" She pointed the light up the stairs that led to the ninth floor. By the sixth floor, they'd realized that the linen closet was in the same place on each floor. But when they reached the ninth floor, they found its linen closet was empty, too.

"Now what?" asked Joe.

"I guess we look elsewhere," Nina replied.

They looked at Bob. He shrugged. "I can't think of anything else."

They walked down the hallway and started back down the stairs. Joe and Nina had reached the seventh floor before they realized that Bob wasn't with them. They turned quickly, Nina shining the beam up the stairs.

Bob stood at the top, his lips pressed together in thought.

"What's wrong, Bob?" Joe asked.

Bob didn't reply. He only stood and stared. Then he began nodding his head up and down.

"What's wrong with him, Joe?" Nina said.

"I don't know," Joe answered. "I've never seen him like this."

Bob's head nodded several times, then stopped. Then he nodded a few more times and stopped again. He did this two more times. Then a big smile spread across his face. He looked down at his friends.

"Come with me," he said, crooking his finger at them.

"Are you sure? Tell us what's going on," Nina said.

"Come with me," Bob repeated. Then his voice deepened into a bad European accent. "Come, my children of the night." He disappeared up the stairs.

"Bob!" Nina called.

Joe darted up the stairs after his friend.

"Joe!" Nina shouted. She grunted, then gave up and followed them.

They found Bob at the end of the hallway on the ninth floor. He was leaning into the wall, his head turned to the side, his ear pressed against the paneling.

"This is no time for kidding around, Bob," Nina said.

"Shh!" Bob said, a finger raised to his lips.

"What is it?" Joe said.

"How many floors have we explored?" Bob said.

"I don't know," Nina replied.

"Nine," Joe said.

"Nine floors," Bob repeated. "Nine floors." He stepped back from the paneling. "Nine floors." He took a deep breath and then kicked out with his right foot. The panel splintered. Bob kicked it again and again until a large hole appeared.

Nina pointed the flashlight through the hole to reveal a set of stairs.

"But the Carfax has ten floors of rooms," Bob said. "Shall we?" He bowed a little and waved his arm toward the stairs.

"You're a genius, man," Joe said, stepping through the hole. Nina sighed and followed.

They walked in unison up the tenth flight of stairs. When they reached the top, they cautiously approached the linen room. Bob flung open the door, ready to battle the Lord of Darkness himself.

Nothing. The room was empty.

Bob frowned.

"Nice try," Nina said. She glanced down the hallway and screamed.

Joe and Bob ran to her side. Nina's flashlight illuminated the figure of Devin, floating several inches above the floor. Her pale skin was a stark contrast to the black dress she was wearing. Her lips were bloodred and her long black hair floated about her like the snakes of Medusa.

"You have come for the ceremony," Devin said, her voice distant and metallic. "The Master will be pleased. He is a bit of a egotist and likes to have an audience. Come. Come." She smiled, revealing long, pointed canine teeth. "It is about to begin." She turned and floated down the hallway.

"What do we do?" Bob asked

"We're here," Joe replied. "Let's find out what this ceremony is all about, and how Devin suddenly learned to defy gravity."

They followed Devin down the hallway.

"Devin," Nina said. "What are you doing here? I thought Abel — I mean, Dracula — took you home."

Devin laughed. "The Count and I returned when you three left. Angela was here, waiting."

"Waiting for what?" Nina said.

"Waiting for this."

They reached two large oaken doors. Devin fanned her hands out and the doors opened, unaided.

Nina, Joe, and Captain Bob stepped into a large ballroom bathed with flickering torchlight. Devin floated a few more feet into the room and then sunk slowly to the floor next to another figure, whose head was bowed. The figure's head raised slowly, revealing a pale face translucent with veins.

"Angela!" Nina said, gasping.

Angela was dressed in a bloodred wedding dress. Her eyes were closed. A black choker with a silver dragon clasp encircled her neck. She looked like a life-sized porcelain doll.

"Welcome!" said a deep foreign voice that reverberated through the ballroom. "Welcome!"

Nina pointed her flashlight to a corner of the room. It was Dracula. His open, broad smile revealed teeth that came to a sharp point.

"Welcome, my children." He floated toward Devin and Angela. "You are just in time." He settled next to Angela and took her hand. Angela shuddered visibly.

"In time for what, you bloodsucker?" Bob said loudly.

Dracula shot a look of pure hatred at Bob. Then he smiled again. "In time for my union with my eternal love." He kissed Angela's hand. She shuddered again.

"Union?" Joe said.

"He plans to marry her," Nina said.

"Florida requires a blood test, buddy," Bob said.

"Interesting choice of words," said Dracula with a laugh.

"Whoops," Bob said softly.

"Smooth move, Captain Boob," Nina whispered.

"I have searched through all eternity for my lost love," Dracula said. "Never did I dream that I would find her in another world and another time. Your Angela is my lost angel."

"Do you know what he's talking about?" Nina whispered.

"This wasn't in the movie," Bob replied.

"Silence, you heretics!" Dracula's voice filled the room.

"I think," Joe whispered, "that Dracula believes Angela is his soul mate and he intends to marry her so they can be joined forever."

"You are correct," Dracula said. He stroked Angela's blond hair. "And my love and I will rule a world of vampires, and the living will be our slaves." He turned to Nina, Joe, and Bob. "When I first came into your world, I was attacked by a boy. He had a photograph of a lovely maiden, the girl you call Angela. She belongs not to your world but to my ancient and immortal world. And I had to find her. Do you believe in destiny?"

"I believe that people ought to have a right to choose their destinies," Nina replied, her eyes flashing.

"Some destinies are carried along the winds of time like a leaf in a storm," Count Dracula said.

"Typical adult," Bob said. "Here comes the lecture."

"Silence, infidel!" The vampire thrust his hand forward, palm out. He was a good ten feet from Bob, but Bob felt as though a steel fist had smashed into his chest. He sprawled backward onto the floor.

Dracula hovered around Angela, who stood

motionless. His voice was almost a cry, a plea for understanding. "My lost love lost no longer. The sister of my assistant. The Fates must be on my side. And now we will have a ceremony to unite this eternal love to an immortal life of the undead." He stopped, smiled, and stared at Nina, Joe, and Bob.

"And you three will serve a double purpose. First, as witnesses." Dracula licked his lips.

"And?" Bob said, standing, holding his chest.

"And second — as the wedding feast." He lunged at the trio.

Nina lifted the cross, holding it in front of her flashlight's beam. It cast a giant shadow on Dracula. The vampire screamed, grabbed the edge of his cape, and covered himself.

A shrill shriek filled the air. Devin dove at Nina and knocked her to the ground. The flashlight and the cross flew from Nina's hands and slid across the hardwood floor.

Joe and Bob watched in horror as Dracula leaped up and flew to the rafters thirty feet above the floor, attaching himself to a beam with his clawed feet.

Growling, Devin pounced on Nina. Nina grabbed her by the neck to keep the vampire from reaching her throat with her teeth.

Joe and Bob ran to Nina and yanked Devin off her. Devin kicked and spit at the two. It was all they could do to restrain her.

"Use the water, Nina!" Bob shouted.

"What?"

"Throw the water on her!"

Nina dug into her front pants pocket and pulled out the little bottle of holy water. She flipped the top off and flung the water at Devin. Devin screamed as it hit her in the face, her skin bubbling and crackling as though hit by acid. Devin struggled with the two boys, swinging them around. Nina threw more water on her, hitting her in the face again. Devin screamed and fell to the floor in a dead heap.

A cold wind swept over Nina, Joe, and Bob. They turned in time to see that Dracula had transformed into a giant bat and was swooping toward them. All three fell to the floor just as Dracula glided over them.

"Angela!" Nina yelled. She saw Angela sway back and forth, then collapse. Nina scrambled on her knees to her friend and cradled her in her arms. Angela's eyes suddenly opened, revealing luminous yellow eyes.

"Nina?" Angela said weakly.

"Yes, I'm here," Nina replied.

"Join us!" Angela reached up and pulled Nina closer, opening a mouth full of long, jagged teeth.

"No!" Nina cried, struggling. She lifted the bottle and poured some holy water into Angela's mouth. Angela gagged and coughed.

Nina ripped the black choker with the dragon clasp from Angela's throat. There were two small pencil-sized holes on Angela's neck. Nina poured the remaining holy water on the evil wounds. Angela screamed as the skin bubbled and cracked. And then she fell silent.

"NO!" Dracula screamed from the ceiling. He dropped from the rafter and swooped toward Nina. "YOU WILL DIE!"

Bob ran toward Nina, who was protecting Angela with her own body. He reached into the bag of Communion wafers and pulled out as many as he could, hurling them at the diving Dracula. They hit the vampire and exploded in the air like small bombs.

Dracula let out an angry howl and slammed into the floor, sliding the length of the ballroom and crashing into the far wall.

"Now, Joe!" Bob yelled as he ran to the stunned vampire.

Dracula staggered to his feet, only to be hit by the one-two combination of Joe and Captain Bob. They knocked him off his feet and slammed him into the wall again.

"Now," Bob said, rolling the vampire over.

Joe placed the stake over the center of the vampire's chest and raised the mallet. He brought it down with full force on the stake.

The room exploded in screams from Dracula, Devin, and Angela. What little glass remained in the hotel's windows shattered. The walls shook as though an earthquake had gripped the building.

The wooden floor splintered and cracked. Plaster fell from the wall and ceiling, hitting Nina, Joe, and Bob.

Then all was quiet and still. Bob peeped over his arms.

Dracula lay several feet from him, the stake sticking out from the center of his chest. But it wasn't over yet.

"He's starting to heal himself again," Bob said, picking himself up. "Use the camera now!"

Joe stood up and took the camera from its holster.

Dracula stirred and groaned as the stake began to melt and absorb into his body.

Joe drew closer to the vampire. He flipped open the small viewer. The camera whirred to life. Dracula's image appeared in the view screen.

"Lights, camera, action," Joe said softly. "It's show time!" He pressed the orange RECORD button.

Seconds passed. Nothing happened.

"Move closer," Nina hissed.

Joe inched forward a couple steps.

Dracula groaned. The stake was nearly melted and absorbed into him.

"Closer!" Bob said.

"That's easy for you to say," Joe said, taking a few more small steps toward the vampire.

Suddenly, Dracula rose up from the ground, completely healed. He smiled and slowly began walking toward Joe.

"You have not learned your lesson, my young slave. You have no weapons that can keep me dead. I am not of this world."

"Exactly," Bob said. "And that's why we're giving you a one-way ticket back to your world!"

As Bob spoke, Joe pressed the camcorder's telescopic zoom button. The gears of the lens whirred as the lens lengthened and the image of Dracula grew larger in the viewfinder.

Dracula suddenly stopped. He started to choke. He grabbed his throat. Joe moved closer. Dracula's face filled the small screen.

Dracula fell to the floor and did not move.

"Is he dead?" Nina said, joining Joe and Bob.

"Can the undead be dead?" Bob said.

"Don't you ever stop?" Nina said with a grimace.

"Look!" Joe, still holding the camera on the vampire, pointed to the still figure of Dracula.

A sudden shower of light poured out of the camera. As if in response, a fountain of black, white, and gray shot out of Dracula's prone body like a geyser. The stream hit the ceiling and fell to the ground in a cascade of color. It splashed like water across the ballroom floor.

"Look out," Bob shouted. He ran for the nearest table and leaped on top.

Joe and Nina just watched, paralyzed, as the solution ran about their feet and outlined the bodies of Angela and Devin.

Dracula's body slowly collapsed. Like flesh in

acid, the body melted and became part of the pool of color. The pool began to swirl slowly, then faster, forming a whirlpool. Nina and Joe backed up toward the wall as the pool grew larger in concentric circles.

"What's happening?" Nina shouted.

"We've seen this before," Joe said. "Remember? The night of the storm, when the projector blew up."

The vortex of light grew and grew until it reached a diameter of six feet. Then, with a great sucking sound, the liquid was vacuumed through the lens and into the camera.

"Cut and print. That's a wrap!" Bob declared.

CHAPTER TWENTY-FOUR
SUNDAY AFTERNOON, THE NEXT DAY

Joe was sitting on the floor in front of the television. He placed the disk in the DVD player and hit PLAY. He scooted back and leaned against the couch.

Bob was relaxing in a recliner while Nina sat on the couch with Angela. They were in Joe's living room.

The word *Dracula* appeared on the screen in bold white letters. They waited through the credits and the movie's opening scenes. It didn't occur to any of them to punch the SEARCH mode on the DVD and advance the movie forward.

"There he is!" Bob shouted, startling the others.

Count Dracula appeared in all his evil, black-and-white glory.

"You mean to tell me that Count Dracula was transported from this old movie into real life?" Angela said, an incredulous look on her face.

"Yes," Bob replied without hesitation. "At first we thought maybe he was a spirit who had taken over a real person's body. It seems, however, that he had been transported into our world with his own identity. He concocted that emergency night dentist ID as a way to explain his nocturnal habits."

"How?" Angela said, doubt in her voice.

"It's a long explanation," Nina said. "Believe me. You'll get a headache if these two guys try to explain it to you."

"Okay," Angela continued. "Dracula escapes, becomes a dentist in San Tomas Inlet, and thinks I'm his long-lost soul mate?"

"Something like that," Bob said, not taking his eyes off the movie. He dug into a bag of microwave popcorn and stuffed his mouth full. "It seems when he attacked Todd, he saw your picture and thought you were Mina Seward, the woman he tried to turn into a vampire in the movie."

"How was Slice involved?" Angela asked.

"That's the part we missed," Bob said, his face reddening. "Remember in the movie, how Renfield first visits Count Dracula and is driven insane? Same thing. Only this time, it was a goofy Goth band leader who thought he could control the real Dracula. Then he thought Dunn was going after Devin, and he tried to stop him."

"You mean Slice actually had feelings for Devin?" Angela asked.

Bob shrugged. "Strange, huh?"

"Very strange. But why did Dracula want me?"

"Apparently," Joe said, "he was looking for similarities between his movie world and the real world. You just happen to have a striking resemblance to the actress who played Mina Seward in the 1931 version of *Dracula*. Not only that, but Dracula learned that he had other powers. For example —"

"You're right," Angela interrupted, turning to Nina. "I am getting a headache!"

"You can't deny what happened," Joe said.

"No," Angela agreed. "But I'm not sure I want to believe your version of events."

"Suit yourself," Bob mumbled through a mouthful of popcorn.

"Whatever the explanation," Todd said, joining the group, "I'm glad you guys got rid of him." He sat next to Angela, who put her head on his shoulder. He smiled and placed his arm around her. "Nuclear popcorn, light on the butter and salt," he said, holding a bag of warm, freshly microwaved popcorn toward her.

"Thanks," she said softly.

"Yeah, this ought to go into *Ripley's Believe It or Not*," Joe said.

"I think the doctors are still amazed at how you and your father recovered so quickly," Bob told Todd. "I wonder how they'd react if we told them that once we sent Count Dracula back to his celluloid world, all the evil he had brought went back with him.

"It's like fiction in reverse," Bob continued. He

207

struck an authoritative pose. "What is reality? What is fiction? How do we know for certain that our dreams are not really reality and our reality merely dreams? Maybe we're not sitting here, now, in this time and place, watching a movie about a fictional vampire. Maybe some kid in some other dimension is watching us watching a movie about Dracula and how we defeated him."

"That's enough, Socrates," Nina said, throwing popcorn at Bob.

"Hey! My mom'll ground me for a month if the house gets messed up," Joe protested.

"To put it in layman's terms," Bob said, picking up the popcorn and gobbling it down (while ignoring Nina's moans of disgust), "all the chaos and destruction and wounds Dracula caused went back with him. They were caused by a fictional character and, therefore, were fictional. As long as Dracula went back to his fictional world, that is. If we'd lost, he could have gone on killing people."

"Where's Devin?" Joe asked. He quickly reached into Bob's bag and grabbed a handful before Bob could pull the bag away.

"She's at the hospital with Slice," Angela said.

Nina rolled her eyes.

"She's going to dump him," Angela explained. "But she doesn't believe in kicking a guy when he's down. He came out of his coma at about the same time Dracula disappeared. His memory of the last month was a total blank. The last thing he remembers is some guy giving him *The Legend of the Vampire* after a show."

"That must be how he put Slice under his influence," Bob added. "That Abel sure was a charming guy. Nina was *really* under his spell." Bob grinned impishly at his friend. She blushed and threw another kernel of popcorn at him.

"Well, we *all* were taken in by him, not just Nina and Devin," Joe pointed out. "Remember how you told him all our theories about the vampire cult, Bob?"

"Oh, yeah," Bob replied, looking embarrassed.

"It must be the legendary charm of the vampire," Nina put in. She was still a little red in the face.

"You and Devin changed back when he disappeared, too," Joe told Angela, tactfully changing the subject.

"I'd like to see what I looked like in a red wedding dress," Angela said.

"Like a she-demon," Bob said quickly.

"*Freshmen!*" Angela threw a pillow at Bob. Bob ducked, plucked a popped kernel from his bag, and tossed it at Angela.

"Hey!" Joe said to Bob. "You're going to vacuum this floor, you yahoo."

"I know the whole thing sounds impossible," Nina said as she stood. "But look at this." She punched the eject button on the DVD player.

Bob and Joe objected, but Nina ignored them. She shoved in a second DVD and hit PLAY. Then she punched the SEARCH button and the movie moved forward quickly.

"See anything missing?" Nina said to Angela.

Angela gazed at the screen, puzzled.

Nina ejected the DVD and put in another one.

"How about this one?"

Angela still didn't answer.

Nina repeated the procedure three more times. Then she shut off the television and stood in front of Joe, Bob, Angela, and Todd, her arms folded across her chest.

"All the monsters are missing from the movies Joe had transferred to the special DVD format. We put six classic monster movies into the DVD juke-box: *Dracula, The Wolf Man, Frankenstein, The Mummy, Creature from the Black Lagoon,* and *The Bride of Frankenstein.* Now they're all gone from their movies. Except for Dracula. We put him back. But before we put him back, he attacked your boy-friend, Angela, and almost made you and your sis-ter the Mistresses of Darkness. I don't know how to explain it all. I just know it happened. If we hadn't returned him to his world, we'd all be having red wine for dinner, as he liked to put it."

She walked to the picture window and looked out at the ocean.

"We had five other movies in my DVD jukebox besides *Dracula.* And, just as Dracula was once missing from his movie, so the monsters from those five other movies are missing. They've disappeared. Vanished. At least from their reality. If Dracula invaded our world through the bad projector, then we have to assume that the other five monsters are out there. Waiting." She took a deep breath. When she spoke, it was as though she was talking to herself. "Waiting for the right time to attack. And we've got to be ready to stop them. It's got to be us. No one else will believe it."

"We'll have to keep our eyes and ears opened for any unusual paranormal or mysterious occurrences," Joe said. "We need to check the Internet and the news constantly."

Bob stood up and threw on his leather jacket. He zipped it with a determined jerk. He turned slightly so the rest could see the back. "Looks like 'Born to Raze Hell' is taking on a whole new meaning."

EPILOGUE
ONE MONTH LATER

Bob sat at his computer, staring at the screen. He yawned. He had just finished a report on the election of President Benjamin Harrison for his history class. The most boring two hours he had ever spent in his life. The computer's clock showed the time to be 1:00 A.M., but Bob felt as though he had been up for days.

As tired as he was, he wasn't ready to go to bed. He clicked on his dial-up network and waited for the modem to kick in and dial up his ISP. He wished his mother could afford DSL.

Once on-line, Captain Bob clicked on his favorites list and scrolled quickly down to a site that had been helpful in the past.

His eyes quickly scanned the headline links:

TWO-HEADED BOY WINS RACE BY A NOSE

SCIENTIST DISCOVERS SECRETS OF PROCRASTINATION:
WILL RELEASE RESULTS AT A LATER DATE

ALIENS SAID TO BE LIVING AMONG US
AS CIVIL SERVANTS

LAW OF GRAVITY DECLARED UNCONSTITUTIONAL

He scrolled through the headlines, hoping to find the most unusual item for his Current Events class. He needed the article for extra credit. He had let his grade fall to a 69, and Mr. Hepner, his Current Events teacher, had told him that he could get ten extra-credit points for each unusual news item he could find. This site had been a grade-saver more than once.

He vision blurred and his eyelids begged to be closed. Bob had to force them open more than once.

Then his eyelids shot open when he saw the following headline:

WEREWOLF ATTACKS RODEO QUEEN

He scanned the article as quickly as he could read.

The first thing to catch his eye was that the event happened in Florida, in a small town called Wales, about fifty miles to the west of San Tomas Inlet.

The second thing to catch his eye was the number of cattle mutilations that had occurred near this small town.

The third and last thing to catch his eye was that

several witnesses had reported that a giant wolf had attacked the cattle and other animals in the area, and had even attacked a local rodeo queen.

One witness was adamant that the creature was not merely an overgrown wolf, but a creature straight out of the deepest fears of human kind's nightmares. He insisted that a werewolf had invaded central Florida and only the devil himself could send his canine hellhound back to hell.

Bob finished reading the article and sighed. He clicked on the print icon. His ink-jet printer hummed to life.

As the pages of the Internet article shot out of the printer, Bob picked up his cordless phone and dialed Joe's telephone number. He knew that his buddy would be upset that he was calling so late.

He cradled the phone between his ear and his shoulder. The phone began chirping on the other end. Captain Bob adjusted the yacht cap on his head. He picked up a slim DVD box: *The Wolf Man*.

Forget about the extra credit for Current Events, Captain Bob thought, *we've got a werewolf to battle in Volusia County!*

About the Author

Since childhood, Larry Mike Garmon has been an aficionado of things that go bump in the night. Watching such classic horror movies as *Frankenstein* and *Psycho* added to his anxiety about strangers with glowing eyes. Reading horror comic books and tales of terror from Edgar Allan Poe, Nathaniel Hawthorne, H. P. Lovecraft, and Ambrose Bierce compounded his concern, but also encouraged him to try writing scary stories of his own. He often listens to Bach and Metallica while writing his creepiest scenes.

Larry Mike lives with his wife, Nadezhda, in Altus, Oklahoma. They have five children — three grown and two still in school. Larry Mike is an English teacher at Altus High School, while Nadezhda is a pianist and vocalist. They have two dogs, two cats, and a vintage 1965 Buick Wildcat.

Although Larry Mike still enjoys a good horror movie or novel, he says there is nothing more horrifying than teaching a room full of teenagers! He is an active member of the Horror Writers Association, and can be reached at MonsterMan@LarryMike. com.

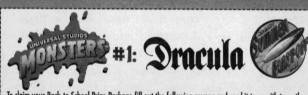